Sarah Tytler

Saint Mung's City

A novel. Part 2

Sarah Tytler

Saint Mung's City
A novel. Part 2

ISBN/EAN: 9783337052362

Printed in Europe, USA, Canada, Australia, Japan

Cover: Foto ©Andreas Hilbeck / pixelio.de

More available books at **www.hansebooks.com**

A Novel

By SARAH TYTLER

AUTHOR OF 'THE BRIDE'S PASS,' 'WHAT SHE CAME THROUGH,'
'BEAUTY AND THE BEAST,' ETC.

IN THREE VOLUMES

VOL. II.

London

CHATTO AND WINDUS, PICCADILLY

1884

CONTENTS OF VOL. II.

CONTENTS.

SAINT MUNGO'S CITY.

CHAPTER XIII.

THE COMMON ENEMY.

THAT winter there was one of the most terrible outbreaks of typhoid fever, which had stricken Rory of the Shelties, ever known in St. Mungo's City. The sickness extended to the suburbs, and sent long arms into the country, reaching to the Aytoun Water, which was so valuable an auxiliary of Drysdale Haugh, creeping up and down its banks in foul malaria, which prostrated alike strong men and weak women, robbed families of their bread-winners, or slew the strapping lads and blooming lasses who were the hope and pride of elderly fathers and mothers.

There was no doubt the first signs of the plague had made their appearance after the excesses and exposure of the Fair week. There had been no spell of short hours and starvation wages to induce such a low state of body and mind as to form a fit foundation for the mischief. But whatever its origin, it soon extended far beyond the defaulters whose deeds had wrought their doom. The fever, after a certain course, appeared to strike impartially the sober, industrious workman, and the idle, dissipated hanger-on for a day's ' turn ' to relieve his most pressing wants. The evil rose in the scale of society, and fell upon the well-to-do, scattering sickness and distress among the rich, while naturally its vantage-ground was the quarters of the poor. It clove to them as to its fitting haunts, and, like a cowardly assailant, did deadliest injury where there was least power of resistance.

It was a busy time for Dr. Peter and Athole Murray, who acted from the first as her father's indefatigable assistant, feeling no fear to go on the call of duty where he went with his life in his hand, day and night.

Auld Tam took the greatest interest in the nature of the outbreak, and showed not the slightest shrinking from a contact with which, indeed, he had been familiar in his early days. It was a mortification to him to discover that his best cottages were not spared; but he fell back on the comfort that there the remedies were applied with the least difficulty and the greatest average of success.

But the tug of war came when the epidemic raged so fiercely in the worst Glasgow slums that it roused an apathetic public. Tam Drysdale was not the man to stand and gape and groan or merely moralize or sermonize over the calamity, far less was he the heartless egotist who

would employ his resources to flee from the
foe, leaving a helpless multitude in its
clutches.   He was ready to fight it hand
to hand, as he had fought all the early
obstacles in his career.   He was not only
foremost in appointing and attending meet-
ings of men in high enough places to cope
with sanitary mischief; but when a house-to-
house visitation was started, he, who might
have pleaded that his interests were at
Drysdale Haugh, was one of the first to put
down his name as a visitor in the darkest
places of the city.   His strong firm step
was the readiest to enter the infected dwell-
ings, where there was not a breath of air
that was not heavy with poison.   He was
known to pull off his coat, on an emergency,
and carry a patient—a man mad with de-
lirium, whom it would have required two
ordinary men to master—on his back from
one room to another; and where he found
none save exhausted, half-distracted women
to watch the sick, he sometimes sent the

watchers to bed, and took their vigil till some other good Samaritan relieved him in turn.

Every morning the two Eppies—not to be deceived, knowing too well the expeditions on which auld Tam was bent—clung to him at parting with prayers and tears. He put the woman and the girl gently from him, and went his way; and on his return, for the first time in his life, he would not permit them to hang about him till he had passed through such processes of bathing and changing his clothes as should ensure his wife and daughter's safety. His obduracy would have half-broken their hearts if the stayers at home had not been encouraged to be as busy as bees in Tam's absence, concocting such stores of jellies and soups, and manufacturing such loads of sick-room clothes, as not the most accomplished cook and housekeeper in the world could have achieved single-handed—even if she had condescended to employ her talents day after day—not for the dining-room or the linen-presses at Drysdale Hall, but for afflicted sections of the Gallowgate and the Sautmarket.

The strait was so great that everybody with time and means and a heart to feel was called into requisition. Neither did Claribel Drysdale refuse to obey the call, but she worked in the ranks of Lady Semple, to whom she was an available auxiliary, while the two Eppies were sufficient for themselves at home.

The first thing that staggered Tam Drysdale was stumbling on his son Tam engaged in the same work as himself. The father's hale colour sensibly paled, and a troubled look came into his eyes.

'What are you seeking here, Tam?' he asked almost roughly. 'This is not a place for a student fellow like you. You are not used to the ways of the poor folk: you'll only add to the trouble if you come to grief; you can do no possible good. Go home to your books, but take care you do not come near your mother and sisters in that coat and these breeks.'

Young Tam looked his father more fully in the face than he had done for some time, with more of an answering challenge in the brown eyes which were so like his mother's in tint, and yet had his father's determined glance. There was no sullenness in Tam's face at this moment—rather a sense of grim amusement and something that might have stood for fellow-feeling.

'I'm not such a mere bookworm as you think me, sir. How should I not know the ways of the working people, among whom I have dwelt all my life? I'll not come to grief any more than you will. What are *you* seeking here, may I ask, father?'

'Don't talk nonsense, Tam,' said his father testily; 'you know it is my place, as the maister of a public work, to see into the condition of the people, both here and

at Drysdale Haugh, on an occasion like the
present. Forbye, I am familiar with the
situation. I mind the last bad outbreak of
the fivver. It was when I was in my
'prenticeship and staying with my uncle
Geordie. There were five in the hoose laid
down with it. My cousin Nancy deed,
poor lass! and there was nobody to look
after Sandy during the night, and keep him
from louping over the windy, but me. I
had a regular training to such scenes.'

Young Tam hesitated for a moment.

'I have not quite understood hitherto
what duties a master's position is supposed
to include,' he said at last, a little stiffly;
'but if I am ever to undertake them, I
should say my training had better begin.'

Auld Tam's whole aspect brightened in-
describably.

'Plenty of time for that,' he said gruffly,
but heartily, 'and your experience should
come by degrees, Tam, not in a dunt
[sudden blow], as it comes to working lads

bred hardily as I was, and called to face
the best and the worst all round from the
beginning. It is not easy, but it is in the
day's work—part of their lives. Besides,
they say,' added Tam hastily, 'the fivver
is more catching for the young than for the
auld.'

'You're not old,' said young Tam hastily,
with a quick sharp denial that sent a
glow through his progenitor's veins. 'You
are hardly middle-aged. People should
call stages of existence by their right
names.'

'Anyway, I'm auld Tam when you are to
the fore,' said his father, much as he would
have spoken to his daughter Eppie, 'and
it is richt the young should be spared to
take the place of the auld.'

'It is nothing of the kind,' answered
young Tam doggedly. 'Take your place!
very likely. I wonder which would be most
missed. You know very well, father, you
could ill be spared. You ought not to run

risks like these, while it does not matter for a fellow like me.'

'Lad, you are tempting the Almighty!' cried Tam almost fiercely; 'are you so left to yoursel' as to think you could well be spared by your mither—and me?' he ended with a gulp of the words, and a grip as of iron of young Tam's shoulder. 'But it is all nonsense!' he said, putting force upon himself the next moment. 'We've got a trick of disagreeing; that is what it is.'

'And I am afraid there is little prospect of our doing anything else, if the alternative is my keeping out of Glasgow, and your going on as you have been doing for the last ten days,' retorted young Tam, defying his father openly.

And auld Tam gave in with the moisture in his eyes, and his hand still on his son's shoulder.

'Well, well,' he said, 'have it your own way, laddie; you've always been as kittle [ticklish] to deal with as a woman, Tam—

far worse than your sisters. But if we sail
in the same boat for once, it will be some
sma' comfort.'

The sailing in the same boat through a
crisis of life and death meant from this
moment a certain alteration of tone between
father and son—a certain fraternization—
temporary, and only on one point as yet,
but never entirely lost sight of in their
subsequent differences, when young Tam
was born to object, and auld Tam hated
to be contradicted. For one thing, they
saw a good deal of each other during the
next week or two—more than they had
seen since young Tam was a schoolboy.
For another, it was understood between
them that there was a probability of auld
Tam's gaining the desire of his heart, by
his son's becoming, under whatever variety
of opinion, his father's partner and suc-
cessor.

Some of the fever cases in Glasgow were
of the most virulent kind. Occasionally

they assumed the form of the worst sewer-poisoning, from which there was hardly a chance of escape. The inspector of nuisances had neglected his duty. A man and wife—a helpless, handless, poverty-stricken, though honest and sober couple—had been suffered to live, with a large family, in a house which was not fit for a pigsty. First one child sickened, and then another, and died in the briefest interval of time, so that four little bodies were carried away in one hearse, and the expense even of a combined funeral threatened to add starvation to the other pangs of the living. The skin of the last child attacked took green and livid hues before the breath went out of his body.

Auld Tam bent his brows sternly, and swore it was social murder. He half conceived the idea, if he lived and continued to prosper, of doing something more than found a family, and bring Drysdale Haugh to perfection—something to atone for the neglect by the better endowed and better informed of the less qualified and more ignorant—something in which young Tam might be with him heart and soul, till Glasgow should speak of the father and son, as, indeed, they were speaking of them at this moment, though auld Tam paid no heed to it.

The fever, as it raged, was turning up in the more respectable quarters, in the old squares and streets, where the houses were good and spacious, but the drains had been little thought of, and the sun seldom shone.

Young Tam Drysdale saw his father at the office one afternoon, and remarked with consternation that he looked as if he had received a shock to his whole system—at the same time he was deliberately delaying the ordinary hour of his return to Drysdale Hall. He pooh-poohed the idea of anything wrong with him physically, or of rest being desirable, at the very moment that he was moving about in a perturbed manner,

showing signs of trouble and perplexity in
every line of his usually strong, sagacious
face.

'Shut the door, Tam; I do not want
those fellies out there to catch a sough
[murmur] of what I have got to say.
Yes, I have come across something that
has grieved me. Grieved is not the word.
Gude Lord! it is enough to shake a man's
faith in the established order of things.
What would your mither think? Her that
was wont to stand in fear and trembling
before such gentlefolks. But, there, she
said, only the other day, that it was a
mystery we should be so weel aff in the
world's gudes, and others as gude—maybe
a hantle better (she's a humble lass, your
mither)—brought to want what they had
been bred to from their cradles. Well, well,
it comes to this, I had speech with one of
the doctors, and he mentioned there were
cases of fever in St. Mungo's Square.'

'So I heard,' said young Tam.

'One of them was an auld Miss Mackinnon, and as I'm a living man, Tam, he added that he did not believe the leddies had enough to eat, though they put the best face on it to him ; and it was a delicate matter to propose to get parish or any other relief for them. The Lord preserve us! the auld Mackinnons—Gavin Mackinnon's aunties, come of the Virginian Mackinnons —to be in want of food, very likely of clothing! Is the end of the world come upon us ? I mind of them being about Drysdale Hall when iheir nephew had it— no very weel-faured [handsome], but gallant, portly, gabby [talkative] leddies, as they had a gude title to be, since they were real edicate leddies for generations back— none of your upstarts that do not know their finger from their thoomb, while they wear silks and velvets. I mind ane of them cracked [talked] like a pen-gun—on things she did not ken muckle about, I must confess, but she had the gift of conversation for

a' that; and another—an aulder woman
than mother is now—played the pianny
better than Clary can do, at a dance and
supper that Mackinnon gave the men before
trips down the water were the order of the
day ; and now to say that the auld leddies
have come to want—Tam, it's seeckening !'

Young Tam had not his father's keen
susceptibilities where real ladies and gentlemen were concerned.   His mind went off
on another tack.

' They must be relations of Mackinnon
who stays so often at Semple Barns.   Why
does he not look after his people ?   I suppose you would call him a real gentleman ?'
suggested Tam, somewhat sardonically.

' It is a burning shame to him !' auld
Tam swore stoutly, ' though a young offisher has not much to spare.   Maybe the
lad does help them, and they are ill mana-
gers, as these gentry often are.   But that
is neither here nor there.   Something must
be done.   I could not sleep in my bed

with such a burden on my mind ; and if
your mither were to hear of it, she would
not break bread for the next twal' hours.
I want you to come along and call with
me, Tam. We can pass ourselves off as
sent on an inspection among great and small
throughout the town. The leddies cannot
be going much about to hear the story contradicted. We can see and judge for ourselves. And it may be possible to put in
a word about the superiority of country pro-
visions, and whether the Miss Mackinnons
would do me the honour to accept a speci-
men of meat and dairy produce and vegetables and fruit from Drysdale Hall. I
think it might be managed in that way,
and the favour could be repeated. I have
been turning over in my mind whether I
could not get up an auld debt to Ganvin
Mackinnon, but sic a lee would stick in my
throat; then the young lad Mackinnon
might interfere, and detection would be
awkward.'

'Upon my word, father, I never knew you were so accomplished a deceiver,' said young Tam, grave as he was, unable to keep from laughter. 'I never thought to pay visits with you under false pretences.'

'Do not gibe, Tam,' said his father, as solemnly as he would have rebuked a jest at a death-bed. 'This is not a subject for gibing. You heard what the doctor said— it is a most delicate matter to ask leddies to take anything save a parcel of idle compliments from you. If stratagems are ever allowable, it must be here.'

Indeed, death was very near, in more shapes than one, to the old stripped house in St. Mungo's Square. It was Miss Bethia, the youngest and the most able-bodied sister who had been smitten, and when she was 'sooming [swimming] for her life,' as Miss Janet admitted brokenly, the chief source of livelihood for the other sisters was withdrawn from them. The moment the disease had declared itself, Miss Janet had written to her grand-nephew, forbidding him to come near the house on account of the infection. He broke through the prohibition, but he never got beyond the front-door, where Miss Janet consented to parley with him, solely on condition that he held his handkerchief to his mouth and did not cross the doorstep.

Such aid as the Lieutenant sent consisted of trifling delicacies, while, alas! there was dismal lack of the commonest necessaries.

While Miss Bethia was at the worst, it seemed that her sisters needed little more food than sufficed for the sick-room. They lived upon their anxiety—hope and fear acted as stimulants to them. It was when the patient had got the turn, and required more nourishment than milk and beef-tea, that the exhausted state of Miss Janet and Miss Mackinnon began to show itself plainly. But as people can grow accustomed to abstinence up to a certain point, and cease to feel the cravings of appetite, after they have

22—2

failed by degrees to be appeased in anything save the most partial and perfunctory
manner, so the feeble, shaky, but still
dauntless scarecrow, Miss Janet, preserved
an attitude of heroic stoicism throughout
her interview with the two Drysdales.

Miss Janet had two motives to nerve her
to endure to the end. She had never quite
forgiven Tam Drysdale for having succeeded
her late nephew at Drysdale Haugh ; therefore he was the last man in Glasgow to
whom she would have consented to be be-
holden in the direst extremity. It made no
difference that the grudge was groundless
and utterly unreasonable. That was one
link in the argument ; another, and still
stronger, turned on the fact that if she
ever consented to waive her displeasure and
accept the overtures of the Drysdales, it
must be, as before, on the plea of a marriage,
and she was not going to spoil Eneas's
chances by betraying the poverty of the
land in St. Mungo's Square. No ; there

were still some potatoes and oatmeal in the larder, and Miss Janet felt as independent as Andrew Marvel with his mutton-bone.

Miss Bethia might have behaved differently, when she lay on her bed, weakly crying, with the stirrings of new life in her, and the promptings of a child's fresh hunger, never satisfied; but she would have been the first to feel ashamed of her infirmity when strength was restored to her.

Tam Drysdale was nearer to breaking down in his manliness than he had been in the whole course of his life, when he sat in the bare wreck of a room, without a fire, on the chill autumn day, waiting for the appearance of one of the ladies. He kept muttering, half under his breath, ' Gude Lord, Tam !' and, ' Have the leddies come to this ?' He ' thought shame ' when he recalled the prized grandeur and substantial comforts and luxuries of Drysdale Hall. He rubbed

his forehead, and screwed up his courage
for the carrying out of his mission.

When Miss Janet entered, Tam's heart
was wrung anew. He would never have
known his old acquaintance—the gallant,
portly lady of the past—in the fallen away.,
haggard woman in the old-fashioned garments, that looked so much too wide, they
appeared to flap about the big-boned figure ;
only the remembered 'gabbiness' of the
lady remained as a present trait. For if
Miss Janet did not receive her late nephew's
former servant with 'becks and bows and
wreathed smiles,' she treated him and his
son with a kind of brow-beating condescension. She made her explanations with
wonderfully little cutting short of her long
tongue, considering the small amount of
fuel in the form of nourishment it and
the rest of her bodily powers had to work
upon. But the voice was at once weaker
and shriller in what *timbre* it possessed,
and a little faltering occasionally, while a

tremulous movement passed from time to time over the hard-favoured features; and the worn hands, which she had not been sufficiently mistress of herself to encase in gloves, shook beyond the power of control as they lay in her lap.

Miss Janet said she and her elder sister had been sitting in poor Betheye's room, and had dispensed with a fire elsewhere. Betheye was doing very well now. Oh yes! she had every advantage—a good doctor, and her grand-nephew the Lieutenant was constantly sending fruit, and what not. They—the Miss Mackinnons—felt for the poor sufferers from the sickness. It was quite right a fund should be raised for them. She would look about, when she had time, and see if she could find any odds and ends that might be useful. She spoke as if she and hers were as far removed as the Drysdales themselves from the deprivations and dependence of poverty.

Young Tam had never seen his father so deferential as to this 'genteel, half-crazy object of charity,' the younger man was guilty of calling poor Miss Janet. It was with absolute trepidation and a doubly-respectful 'Miss Mackinnon, mem,' that auld Tam delivered the sentence he had laboriously composed of the excellent unadulterated character of all articles of food in the country, and the comfort to be derived from availing one's self of them in an unhealthy season. This was the prelude to a petition that Miss Janet would permit him to send her 'a basket from Drysdale Haugh which might remind her of "auld lang syne."'

Perhaps the reference was not very happy; anyhow, Miss Janet gave a quavering laugh, and told him she was greatly obliged, but he must not trouble himself. The town and the country were brought so near now, they were equally well supplied with victuals of every description; she and her sisters had all they could wish. She did not think even the Strathdivie curds and cream, new-laid eggs, and stubble chickens could taste better than what could be found in Buchanan Street. She remembered hearing that her grandfather would always have fowls from Strathdivie when he wanted cockie-leekie or hen-broth, but farm troke [goods] were rife everywhere now. She would offer the gentlemen wine (there was only a thimbleful in Miss Bethia's room), but she understood from her grand-nephew that it was not the fashion now to taste anything after luncheon; so Miss Janet, with flying colours, dismissed the intruders. Neither father nor son was in the least degree deceived, and young Tam, at this stage, felt as little inclined to gibe as his father.

'The puir leddy is reduced to skin and bane,' said auld Tam, with a groan. 'I do not believe she has had butcher meat, or any other support than a bit bread and

a blash [watery mixture] of tea, for a
month. If we do not get the better of her
quickly, she'll be past the reach of mortal
man. And there are three of them—one
just out of the fivver—in the same plight.
Gude Lord! something must be done.
Shall we drive to the Barracks and break
the story to that careless puppy of an
offisher? It is for him to interfere, and
not suffer his aunties, who brought him up,
to perish, though he has to force meat and
drink down their craigs [throats].'

Certainly, if no other resource could be
hit upon, Eneas Mackinnon must be appealed to, however painful the appeal to
both parties.

But young Tam had another idea which
might obviate the disagreeable step, for the
present at least.

' The Mackinnons and Murrays were old
acquaintances when Gavin Mackinnon and
Dr. Peter's father were partners. Send in
Dr. Peter to see the ladies, as a piece of

attention from an old friend. That will
save them the expense of further medical
attendance, if it does nothing else, and he
will make his observation and deliver his
report.'

Auld Tam was only too thankful to take
his son's advice, and secure another coad-
jutor in the ticklish business.

CHAPTER XIV.

ATHOLE MURRAY COMES TO THE RESCUE.

DR. PETER, in the middle of his work, responded readily to the call. It proved that he had not only known the Mackinnons in his youth; he had always kept up some intercourse with them, and Athole had been in the habit of calling in St. Mungo's Square occasionally. He looked grave and resolute when he saw Tam Drysdale by appointment afterwards. Yes, the poor old ladies were at the wall, sure enough; and even viewing the matter in a professional light alone, something must be done immediately, or there would be more than one death to answer for. But he had his proposal ready. Athole must take up her abode in St. Mungo's Square for a week or two, till Miss Bethia was able to be removed for change of air to Barley Riggs. Only a woman could cope with the circumstances where women were concerned, and he had paved the way for his daughter's arrival. He had told Miss Janet that he wanted a little change for Athole, asked if she—Miss Janet—would take in the girl for a while, and hinted at a board. The old lady, with her instincts of hospitality, her necessities, and her pride, had been too bewildered to make any decided opposition. Now he would not stand on further ceremony; he would act as if he took Miss Janet's and her sister's consent for granted, despatch Athole the next morning, and when she was once in the house, it would be hard for the Miss Mackinnons to turn her out. Athole would bring the sinews of war, and would propose to undertake the housekeeping on the plea of relieving the sister-nurses, who were too weak and worn out to make any effectual resistance.

Auld Tam as he listened, stared fixedly at Dr. Peter.

'But, man, she's your dochter, your last-hame lassie, the very apple of your eye,' he remonstrated, with wonder and rising vehemence. 'I ken what Tam and little Eppie and Clary are to me, and I have their mither —that I sometimes say is worth them all— while you have only this lassie left at hame; and you are sending her where the fever has just been, and where a great burden of responsibility, work, and fatigue will fall upon her young shoulders.'

'I know,' said Dr. Peter, bowing his head as if sealing a bargain. 'But did you never think, Tam, that the way to keep a thing you prized was to give it freely in the name of God and your neighbour? I never would shut Athole out of the way of the fever, when she could be of use. She had no fear, and I believed I could take care that she ran little more risk than if she had stayed locked up in the parlour at Barley Riggs. I was right, and you'll see I'll be right again. You may trust me to take care of Athie,' he ended, with a smile.

' But what if you should be mistaken, Peter ?' Tam felt bound to press the point. ' If an accident were to happen, if you were to lose your lassie by her foolhardy exposure'?

' There is no foolhardiness, and there is very little exposure,' maintained Dr. Peter unflinchingly ; ' not more than happens to every doctor and nurse—indeed less, for I shall be always in the background, ready to step in at the first note of warning. And if it were to come to the worst, Tam,' he said slowly, with a peculiar light coming into his eyes, ' what then ? It would be the will of God. It is given to every man and woman once to die ; nothing—not all the love and care in the world—can prevent the execution of that sentence. And can

death come better to any man or woman
than in the way of duty ?   I know what is
in your mind—it is not of the one to be
taken, but of the one left behind, you are
thinking.   Well, what is to come of somebody's journey might be shorter, as the road
would be darker—that is all—not so very
much when the day is far spent and its work
three-fourths done.'

'Peter Murray, I honour you with all my
heart,' said auld Tam warmly ; ' but I could
not do it, man—I could—not—do it.   It is
with no will of mine that young Tam is in
the thick of this fray ; but he's man-grown,
with a mind of his own.   I'll not say that
it has been all loss that I've seen a bit of
the lad's mind lately, and we've focht together against the fivver—young Tam and
me ; only the price might have been ower
heavy, God help me ! and I could not have
sent him into the battle, or even given my
consent to his entering the ranks, if he had
condescended to ask it.   Na, not though it

is the first time since I was a wean that I've had a glimmering that the auld Bible story of Aubraham's offering up his son, his only son Isaac, is more than an allegory or a prophecy, and holds a lesson for men and faithers.'

Auld Tam continued sorely exercised in his mind about the Miss Mackinnons, with Dr. Peter's lassie Athole in the midst of them. To him she was a slip of a young lady whom he knew best as a clever pattern-designer, a bit gentlewoman, with her inalienable rights as such, though neither bonnie nor braw, only as bright as a mavis thrush, as quick as a needle, the charm of whose womanly blitheness and lively wit Tam himself had felt, while he was well aware she was the light of Barley Riggs, the delight of her father's heart. In spite of what Dr. Peter had said, was this a creature to put in the breach, to send to share the privations she was seeking to lighten, and to brave the hardly overcome fever ?

Tam was so troubled in his mind that he
forgot to watch the effect of the news on
his son. He neither saw how young Tam
set his teeth, nor how he reared his head,
and his loss of colour was succeeded by a
warm glow.

Sure enough, if any harm happened to
Athole Murray, it might be laid at the door
of the two Tam Drysdales. Who was it
that had summoned her father on the scene,
and offered a temptation to Dr. Peter's
Quixotic philanthropy?

Both auld and young Tam took it upon
them to go as far as Eneas Mackinnon
had gone—indeed, to go farther, to enter
the hall of the house in St. Mungo's
Square, and solicit speech with Miss
Murray, to hear how her father's scheme
was prospering.

The first time that Athole came down to
the two men, who were together, as she
spoke to them the tears ran down her cheeks
without her knowing it, and she was half

laughing, half crying, though she was not naturally hysterical.

'Oh,' she said, 'I could not have imagined anything like it. If I had guessed a hundredth part of it, I must have got the better of Miss Janet's scruples long ago, though I had let meat and drink down the chimney, as the barber and his wife disposed of the body of the Caliph's favourite in the "Arabian Nights;" I would have come after it was dark, rung the bell, pushed in the basket, and run away. Maybe Miss Janet would have thought the angels or Elijah's ravens had come to her aid. If the Miss Mackinnons had advertised for the owner of that basket they would have been clever if they had found her. Now, we are all right, thank you—at least, we are fast getting right. I open the door, for of course I am the youngest, and the stairs try me least, and I take in all the parcels. If there is anything very suspicious, even for my extensive requirements, I carry it to my room, and Miss Janet is too much of a lady to meddle with what I do there. My father fills the pockets of his overcoat, and has always to speak to me, in private. I can't tell if Miss Janet suspects—I think she must —but her endurance had been stretched to the last thread, and now she submits and ignores my manœuvres. She is so tired that when she has once given in she can't rally her forces for some time. Indeed, my father feared she would either have a bad illness or sink from sheer exhaustion for the first ten days after I came. Oh yes, she's a great deal better, and Miss Mackinnon is pretty well—I am sure Miss Janet must have managed to give her the larger share of the little that was going—and Miss Bethia is progressing favourably. She is by far the most manageable. She and I have quite little feasts in her room.'

'I am most happy to hear it,' said auld Tam, with enthusiasm.

'But, oh! the gaunt emptiness, the

gnawing want, the fainting hopelessness
that must have been in this house!' cried
Athole passionately. 'The mice had de-
serted it months before, Miss Bethia told
me. But Miss Janet and I never speak of
it. We winked at it even when I was
labouring, like a well-disposed brownie, to
fill the cupboards as if they had never
been bare, without anybody witnessing the
performance, and to make a great display of
my accomplishments in cooking—the fruits
of my last lessons at the cooking school.
But I never saw anything at all like what I
beheld first, in the most miserable cottage
at Drysdale Haugh.'

'I sincerely trust you have not suffered
yourself, Miss Murray, mem, from your
great pity and kindness,' said auld Tam,
standing with his hat in his hand before
her.

'I!' she cried incredulously; 'how should
I suffer? It was a bit of an adventure for
me, and I had " a piece in my pocket " all

the time. You know, Mr. Drysdale, the
task was to get older people, more in need
of it, to halve my piece with me.'

Athole had recovered her composure by
the time the next visit of inquiry was made,
and her accounts grew always cheerier and
cheerier, till she began to laugh quite
naturally at young Tam coming alone to
ask for the three Miss Mackinnons, and to
affront him by making game of his odd
contributions to the larder in St. Mungo's
Square, on the whole rather more unsuitable
than the Lieutenant's gifts to his aunts.
' It is not the same as a picnic, Mr. Tom,'
she was at the trouble of explaining to
him.

At last she nearly quarrelled with him by
flatly refusing to take it upon her to have
anything to do with scalloped oysters and
preserved ginger. The Miss Mackinnons
were pretty sure to disapprove of both them
and their donor, and she must also decline
wasting another fraction of her valuable

time in telling him that Miss Bethia's con-
valescence was an established fact, and that
there was nothing the matter with any other
person in the house, while it was too absurd
that he should constitute himself a purveyor
for their wants. He had better go and shop
with his sisters. Oh! *she* did not despise
shopping—she was quite fond of it, when
she had plenty of time and money, and
nothing better to do. If he did not attend
the Nasmyths' ball—the first ball of the
season—the more fool he; the loss would be
his, for she could not flatter him that one
gentleman would be missed, and balls were
excellent things to those who were not
above dancing and making themselves agreeable and useful.

' That is all she thinks me fit for,' he told
himself in a rage; ' she regards me as a
perfect humbug. When she is so grossly
unfair I wonder I trouble myself what she
thinks ; though there is nobody like her that
I know, nobody so good to everybody except

me, so brave and bright—but I will let her
alone in future.'

Miss Bethia was not hard to persuade to
try a change of air at Barley Riggs, and
her sisters were induced to accompany her.
During their absence as much of the old
furniture of the house in St. Mungo's Square
as could be hunted up was restored to it,
without a word said on either side, until its
absence appeared to have been part of an
uncomfortable dream.

The next step was to make Miss Janet
let her name, and the names of her sisters,
be put, in strictest privacy, on the list of
impoverished better-class families helped
by a certain fund. She was led to do so
by being shown the signature of her grandfather among those of the early subscribers
to the fund, and by the facts being impressed upon her that she was only taking
back what he had given. Miss Bethia was,
as Athole Murray had found, by far the
most pliable of the sisters, and she lent

herself half willingly, half with fear and trembling for what Miss Janet would say if she ever found out the unbecoming traffic, to sundry wiles and devices of Athole's, as the instrument appointed by her father and Tam Drysdale for lending the Miss Mackinnons substantial assistance. At the same time Miss Bethia had never received so many or such well-paid orders for work ; altogether, there was hope of the Miss Mackinnons keeping soul and body together till a share of Strathdivie fell to their lot.

CHAPTER XV.

IN the course of the winter the terms of partnership were settled and signed between young Tam and his father, to the immense private satisfaction of the latter, and the innocent jubilation of Mrs. Drysdale. The word 'Son' was added to the halting inscription on the office door. Young Tam began not only to relinquish the college lectures and learned societies to which he had been addicted, in order to stick to the business he had entered upon—he insisted on going back to the beginning and passing through all the preparatory drudgery from which he had till now stood aloof. He wanted to acquire a thorough acquaintance with every stage and department of the business of which he had elected to be one of the masters.

Auld Tam's judgment went with his son's decision. He was in his heart pleased with young Tam, and proud of him for his resolution. The senior partner rejoiced to see the junior in an office coat, or even in a dyer's suit, more than he had ever magnified him in a dress-coat among his peers; yet the father would have willingly spared the son any ordeal that could well have been avoided. He would have treated young Tam's early reluctance to become a dyer and calico-printer, now that it was overcome, with the greatest delicacy, dealing gently with the deficiencies which were likely to be its fruit. Auld Tam dreaded the young man's becoming soured at the outset, and turned beyond recall, in his heart, against the business, though his father had enough confidence in him to feel sure that he would keep his word and

the terms of the partnership. He would
be nominally 'son' in a business sense,
though he had lost all save a pocket
interest in the matter, and though he
ended by being the veriest of sleeping
partners raised up to serve as a tool for
rogues.

But young Tam doggedly declined to
suffer himself to be spared. He was one
of the few people who, in the course of
every fault and blunder they commit, when
punishment is going, choose to punish
themselves first and most, and derive a
grisly solace from such atonement as can
be afforded by the hard lines the culprits
compel themselves to endure. But it is '
not a pleasant process to go against the
grain, and swallow huge mouthfuls of irk-
some details in a cause that is apt to look
like nothing better than mercenary enterprise. The worst does not turn to the
best, to the brave, at once.

There are many things to be taken into

consideration. There is a natural reaction from the exalted mood in which a man gives up his will and makes what appears to him a signal sacrifice, which includes the subsequent depression, mortification, and irritation with which he finds he has not counted all the cost, and is hardly equal to the payment of the pound of flesh. Hitches are certain to occur in late concessions. Among the hitches are the lurking jealousy and latent malice of subordinates who have been disappointed in little schemes of their own, and do not want a new master.

In addition, young Tam Drysdale's temper was not of the best; and although he was perfectly sincere in what he was about, he did not accomplish his transformation into a man of business altogether gracefully or graciously. It was far from being uninterruptedly smooth water in the Glasgow office, and at the Drysdale Haugh vats and bleaching-greens in those days;

yet auld Tam was wonderfully forbearing, and young Tam, having once given in his adherence to his natural destination, practically kicked against it no more.

There was a considerable amount of gaiety this year, as there always was in winter among the young people of the Drysdale set, notably among Clary's peculiar allies. Dick Semple was much at home, and his friend Eneas Mackinnon was frequently with him. Lady Semple had a couple of young ladies, English cousins, paying her a visit, whom she turned over as much as possible to Clary Drysdale, because her ladyship was a busy woman, and because she honestly believed there was a freemasonry between young people which rendered them the best company for each other. Yet there was nothing more conspicuous about Lady Semple—that is to the members of the mercantile class on whom she bestowed her countenance—than the perennial youthfulness of her character.

It was not juvenility of dress and make up,
for she happened to be a woman who cared
little for such things. She said it was
impossible for her to compete with the
Glasgow ladies. She never failed to call
the most dubious specimens on her visiting
list 'ladies'—the mere circumstance of
their knowing her gave them rank so far.
She feared to enter the lists, she declared,
not only in skunk and silver fox, Brussels
point and cut velvet, but in French and
Court millinery. Her old gowns were
comfortable; and her maid fitted her as
well as she cared to be fitted. Lady
Semple wore her own grey hair, though
she was not more than midway between
fifty and sixty. She had never either
powdered or painted in her life. She
patronized bonnets which, whatever else
they did in the way of becoming her,
covered her head. Her mantles were not
tight to her figure, neat and light as that
figure still was for her age. Her nearest

approach to full dress did not go beyond
dinner-dress, and failed to expose her neck
and arms.

When a young woman, Lady Semple
had married a man much older than herself.
She had always been perfectly respectable,
without the smallest taste for the platonic
admiration of a circle of idle young men,
which might explain what even Claribel
Drysdale, who permitted a great deal to
Lady Semple, called her well-bred dowdi-
ness. No competition with other women,
no attempt to attract the attention of any
man save her husband, who gave her *carte
blanche* to dress as she liked, for that matter
hardly noticed how she dressed, accounted
for a good deal.

But whatever youthfulness of person
Lady Semple had early lost, her mind remained as buoyant, versatile, and superficial
as ever. The influence of her husband,
by this time far advanced in age, had not
quenched those attributes in the least. She

was always starting new pursuits, new
systems, new studies, to this day never
doing anything more than skim over the
surface, while she hopped from one to the
other in a fashion most distracting to those
who were not accustomed to her middle-
aged schoolgirl ways.

All the same, Lady Semple was convinced
that she had very little to say to the
Vaughan girls—that, having no daughters
of her own, she had well-nigh forgotten
what young women would care for. On the
other hand, their constant dependence on
her for entertainment would seriously
interfere with her music-practising according to the last Stuttgart method, the
hangings she was working in *appliqué*, her
cottage lectures, her acquisition of dates by
an original method never thought of before.
Claribel Drysdale, who was always disengaged enough to help her friends, would
know what the Vaughans would like.

Clary was nothing loth to become, with

Dick Semple's and Mr. Mackinnon's help,
Lady Semple's representative.   Miss Drysdale was quite willing to introduce the Miss
Vaughans to everything and everybody they
might care to know, in a sphere rather
different from that to which the daughters
of a well-connected but poor English vicar
had been hitherto accustomed.   Clary was
ready to get up riding-parties, skating-
parties, walking - parties, singing parties,
carpet-dances, for the strangers' benefit.

Perhaps it was somewhat unreasonable
in his sister to expect young Tam to join
her in incurring similar trouble, particularly
when the Miss Vaughans presented no attraction to him.   He was overburdened
with worries and weariness from his new
course of life, returning every night from
the office or the Haugh dead-beat, without
confessing it, by engagements which would
have been child's play to his father.   To
the Miss Vaughans young Tam was a surly
Scot—an ungenial if not exactly unmannerly

—for modern manners give great scope for rudeness—mercantile young man.

Florence and Louise Vaughan were neither very young nor very sympathetic. Their standard of duty was framed largely for clergymen's daughters with a view to parish-work. They could tell a good deal with regard to English Church schools, village choirs, and charitable clubs—excellent things to know; but the same judges had few and vague opinions as to what should or what should not be said or done by laywomen, especially by laywomen who were not of the clergywomen's species.

The Miss Vaughans had come to Scotland and Semple Barns, in the immediate neighbourhood of a great commercial city, deeply impressed beforehand with the shocks and surprises the travellers would receive, as if they were about to invade African kraals or Indian wigwams. The new-comers did not miss the sensational

24—2

clement in this visit. They heard a new
language, saw a new style of person, looked
at life from a different standpoint. Not
the least of their discoveries was the abounding wealth which made life so much easier,
and endowed a girl like Claribel Drysdale
with a hundred advantages in dress, amuse-
ments, and power—in a republican world
—of going where she liked, doing what she
chose, and commanding to a great extent
her friends and associates—all with a quiet
mind and a clear conscience. No young
women who were so unfortunate as to
own parents with straitened means, though
the parents' descent was aristocratic, and
their occupations and behaviour unim-
peachable, could hope to attain like
privileges.

The strangers, however restricted their
experience might have been, were not
fools. Their eyes were opened. They
saw what a good thing it was to be
commercially rich, since their mission of

religion not only did not include a vow of poverty, but made no stand against worldliness, so long as worldliness went to daily service, paid respect to saints' days, and decorated the church for festivals.

Lady Semple's cousins were content to accept Claribel Drysdale as a friend. They put due value on her father's carriage, very much at her disposal, her riding-horses, her high-class dress and appointments. Neither was a home like Drysdale Hall left out of the count. It might be over-gorgeous, but it was the perfection of luxury and comfort in its way, where nothing was stinted and nothing grudged. If there were serious objections to Claribel's rustic father and mother, the house was spacious enough; her individual pursuits and engagements were sufficiently respected to allow her to see as little of her near kindred as she chose.

The Miss Vaughans were so won by the material gain that Glasgow trade can produce, they ceased to wonder at their cousin Lady Semple's extending the right hand of fellowship to the wives of those calico-printers, cotton-spinners, and boiler-makers, with whom her husband was on excellent terms. The English ladies went so far as to contemplate the possibility of merging the natural superiority derived from their father's and mother's birth and breeding, name and profession, in com-mercial husbands with the opulence and the indulgence to their wives' whims and fancies which these moneyed men were bound to show.

But young Tam Drysdale did not betray the smallest sign of appreciating Lady Semple's visitors' condescension, or of properly esteeming the severe simplicity of their looks, dress, and ornaments. It was a simplicity which was in honour-able accordance with the Rev. Reginald Vaughan's limited income, but it was not of the same order as Lady Semple's simplicity, being studied and elaborate, where hers was unstudied and careless. Neither was it like that of Athole Murray, which was full of individual character and clever touches.

Young Tam was not vulgar; he had very little of the bagman about him. He had risen above his surroundings still more than his sister Clary had risen above hers. He might pass for a gentleman anywhere. But if he did not happen to be the man for either of the Miss Vaughans, it mattered little, however eccentrically gentleman-like he appeared in other respects.

In lieu of the support of young Tam, Claribel had to fall back on the adherence of Dick Semple and Eneas Mackinnon; though, alas! they were still less eligible in a matrimonial light. Young Tam wanted the will in relation to the Miss Vaughans; but the other two men wanted both the will and the way. Dick Semple had no chance of marrying in his own station without Sir

James's concurrence. Lady Semple had always been easy in her mind about her son, even with regard to Claribel Drysdale, however much they were thrown together, and however friendly the terms on which they stood to each other. For her lady-ship's liberal ideas of fraternization with the families of Glasgow 'bailies,' as she was apt to call them, whether in or out of office, did not extend to proposing to Sir James that his and her solitary chick should quit the ranks of the country gentry to intermarry with sugar or shipping, or Tur-key-red dye, however gilded.

Lady Semple was sure of Dick's senti-ments—that they did not incline in the direction of Drysdale Hall, but in that of a baronial castle, not of yesterday, and still in the hands of a family as old as the time of Queen Mary. Dick did not stoop—he aspired ; and if he persevered long enough, and if no better suitor came for one of several daughters, why, the Semples of

Semple Barns, with a baronetcy of a date not quite so far back as the baron's charters, but not of yesterday either, and an estate as unencumbered as the deplorable condition of agriculture would permit, were not to be despised. Dick might live to have his innings, with the full consent of his father and mother, and of a greater man.

But apart from the Honourable Lilias and Claribel Drysdale, the Vaughan girls, who would never see six and eight and twenty again, and had no looks to speak of, were quite out of the question for Dick.

As for Eneas Mackinnon, to speak of marriage in the same breath with him was a wild absurdity, unless he married a fortune —and every heiress was not so easily attracted by a Mackinnon as poor Maggie Craig had been; while a dowered young lady, unless she drew her dower from the lower walks of trade, was hardly likely to look on the imposing rank of a lieutenant with the reverential eyes of the old aunties

in St. Mungo's Square. Where there were
no fortunes, Eneas Mackinnon, in his youth,
was as much vowed to celibacy as any old
Knight of Malta, any monk among them.

No doubt Claribel might have summoned
to her aid, for the better entertainment
of the Miss Vaughans, other young men,
sons of her father's friends, better inclined
than young Tam or Dick Semple—better
supplied with the means of setting up establishments than Eneas Mackinnon. But
Clary had for a long time hung back a little
from her natural companions. She had no
desire to enter the lists with the Honourable
Lilias. She had not the ghost of a passion for Dick Semple, who, though a good
enough fellow, was still less a man to die
for than Clary had once stated Eneas Mackinnon to be. But though she did not care
in that sense for Dick, she was fantastically
attached to the grade to which he belonged,
even in its farthest ramifications, in preference to her own. She exaggerated the ad-

vantages of the one, and underrated the benefits of the other. She lacked entirely the Miss Vaughans' experience of the stints, shifts, and shams—the unsatisfactory make-believes—of genteel poverty. Clever young woman as Clary was, she showed herself a person utterly ignorant in this respect, while she was willing to stand aside and bide her time, and rather put up with a good many serious objections than relinquish her beau-ideal.

Notwithstanding the drawbacks, the group of young people who had so many appointments together, or in common, presented an attractive enough aspect to lookers-on at Semple Barns and Drysdale Hall, at the meets in the neighbourhood, at the theatre or assembly-rooms, to which Mrs. Drysdale chaperoned them with some trepidation, but abundant kindly good-humour. Claribel Drysdale and her mother were handsome enough in different styles for all the four women. The Miss Vaughans

were supposed to make up by that severely
simple air of theirs for what they lacked in
fairness of face and costliness of apparel.
Some unsophisticated people held that they
were distinguished-looking, because of the
uncompromising absence of the very gifts
and graces which the mass of the assembly
prized and struggled for, and pretended to
have if they did not possess them.

The Miss Vaughans were Lady Semple's
cousins, which meant much in the mercantile community, and their presence at
public places under Mrs. Drysdale's care was
further promotion for her, of which her
daughter Clary was well aware, if the
mother, with her humble-mindedness in
the middle of her gratified vanity, made
little of it.

Poor young Eppie, who was still pro-
hibited from the gaieties of a grown-up
young lady, pined longingly after the people
who had carried off her mother. Eppie
thought Dick Semple, who was thick-set

and plain, quite nice-looking when he wore
his cat's-eye studs, and a bouquet in his
coat; and Eneas Mackinnon an Adonis,
though his studs were of the plainest, and
he had only a couple of ivy leaves, which
Clary had given him, in his button-hole.
The same partial critic considered her
mother, in her velvet and diamonds, and
Clary in her satins and pearls, as 'grand
and lovely.' But Eppie had not much admiration to bestow on Florence and Louise
Vaughan. She did not care for their clinging gauzes, or whatever the material of
their gowns might be; the oxydized silver
girdles, which replaced the austerely plain
leather belts with which the sisters en-
circled the waists of their morning dresses;
the natural flower-trimming for their cor-
sages; the coronals of natural flowers in
their hair. It might all be elegant and
æsthetic, but there was a mummy-like
swathing in the arrangement of the folds,
while the flower-trimmings withered, and

the result was not satisfactory. Unless a
man or a woman was naturally gifted, he
or she had to be trained up to such fashions,
as to the profusion of yellow daffodils
used not long before at a city banquet by
a confectioner of advanced principles of
taste.

'Sheafs of common yellow lilies, auld-
fashioned daffondondillies!' more than one
of the guests had exclaimed in scorn and
derision, feeling himself shamefully balked
of the hot-house flowers to which the price
of his ticket entitled him.

Auld Tam sought to console his younger
daughter left at home.

'Never mind, my lassie, your day will
come. I'll be a proud man when I see you
setting out with mother for your first ball
—you'll make all the other young leddies
stand about.'

'You'll go with me yourself, father, or
I'll not stir a foot!' cried Eppie, recovering
her spirits, and tyrannizing by anticipation.

'But, eh, I wonder young Tam can bide at home. To think he might dance with the best, and that he should stay away to smoke and read. I'm sure he has plenty of time for smoking and reading.'

'Not so much as he was wont to have,' auld Tam corrected her; 'but the felly is well aff if he would but think so; he has a hantle privileges if he would only use them. He is on thrawn [cross] terms with the world, that's what it is, poor Tam!' his father added in a softer tone the next moment. 'For all that has come and gone, will his day ever come?'

'Never mind him, father,' said Eppie cheerfully, 'he's a gowk [fool] not to make the best of his opportunities. He'll come to himself some day, without you troubling your head any more about it. He has gone into the business, and that is something that has pleased mother and you. You'll be my first partner at that ball.'

'Bairn, I would be a fell-like pairtner,' protested Tam, by no means displeased by Eppie's selection. 'I have not danced since I stood up at a kirn [harvest-home]; I believe it was your grandfather's. Your mither was my pairtner, and I dare say she was so far left to herself as to admire my steps, and the cut and shuffle I had learnt for the occasion.'

'You used to dance with me—at least you made me dance and ride when I was a wee thing. Do you not mind how

 ' "Jenny rode to Ru'glen" ?

and

 ' "Shu! shuggie! shug!
   A little birdie in the moss,
   Aneath a bunch o' fug.
   Shu! shuggie! shug!" '

CHAPTER XVI.

THE DINNER-PARTY.

'You'll tak' the high road,
And I'll tak' the low.'

On the greater occasions of the plays and balls, Eneas Mackinnon was given to lounging in the back of the box or about the door of the assembly. He had a sense that he was not wanted. He disliked to be conspicuous; he told himself that he was a detrimental, and accepted the situation with a half-haughty, half-despairing submission. At the home affairs he came out better. It was there that Claribel Drysdale gradually grew to see in him a hero of romance, the only romance that existed for her. She contrasted him favourably with some of the

awkward, engrossed, or pretentious, pre-
suming young Glasgow men. Eneas Mackinnon was never put out in his quietness.
He had plenty of leisure, of which the
ladies he knew, and Claribel Drysdale in
particular, were welcome to avail themselves. He was not at every girl's beck,
yet he was ready to serve women in general
in a way that was very agreeable, and he
was quick to wait upon Claribel in a manner
that had its fascination. He was for the
most part at hand to ride, or skate, or walk,
or dance with Lady Semple's friends or his
own. He was never missing where he
could be of the least use to Claribel Drysdale.

Though Clary was formed to shine in the
society she liked, she had not all the
qualities which render women popular.
Rich man's daughter, and beautiful, quick-
witted girl as she was, she had not been
accustomed to command devotion at once
unobtrusive, unfailing, and unexacting. Be-

sides, the men whom commerce claimed,
even the young men, were not always free
to pay such homage. Eneas Mackinnon's
regimental duty was light and brief compared to the obligations of merchant and
manufacturer. They were all due at their
offices or works on some of the days of
the week, if not on all. The most independent, irresponsible fellows of the number
treated business engagements with great
respect. It was a dogma of St. Mungo's
City, an article of the creed in which they
had been brought up.

Eneas Mackinnon behaved in his proud,
silent manner as if he were nobody, which
somehow made him look so much more
like somebody than the lads whose yachts,
and shooting-boxes, and clubs were never
out of the owners' minds or off their
tongues. He had none of these things,
and still he seemed better without them.
He never took advantage of any favour
granted to him, neither blazoned it forth,

25—2

nor made further advances on the strength
of it, nor refused to vacate his place, on
the least hint, to a better-endowed new-
comer.

Lieutenant Mackinnon, poor, and helpless to better his position, had emphatically
the stamp of one sort of gentleman on him
—not only Dick Semple saw it and chose
him out of all the other officers in their
regiment for his friend : the brusquer young
city men had a perception of the same
attraction. They cultivated Mackinnon's
acquaintance, and paid him the compliment
of looking up to him and copying him in a
good many things; which was a wonder,
seeing that he was next to penniless, and
his admirers by no means steered clear of
the rock of purse-pride in their walk and
conversation.

Of course it was the finer spirits who
were thus moved; the coarser mammon-
worshippers sneered unmercifully at Mackinnon, and at the whole set of empty-

pocketed young officers in the Barracks.
The assailants did their best on all
occasions to bring into strong relief the
assailed's lack of that gear which Glasgow
fathers had picked up for their sons,
about which the said sons puffed and blew,
bragged and hectored.

Attacks of this nature provoked girls like
Claribel Drysdale to stand up in defence of
their partners, and become their determined
partizans. Clary, with her unbounded
regard for gentle breeding, began to get
a little infatuated where the Lieutenant was
concerned, to admire his very laziness,
hopelessness, ponderousness, and powerless-
ness to remedy the misfortune of his circumstances. Though she was quite different,
she sympathized all the more with what
seemed his creed.

'The world is all wrong, but I cannot
set it right, and, indeed, I have not much
confidence in the power of any man to set
it right—an absence of conviction which

leaves me languidly philosophic and gently indolent.'

This is the peculiar form of agnosticism held by young men of the Lieutenant Mackinnon type.

Auld Tam had little respect, but some pity, for young Mackinnon. The present proprietor of Drysdale Hall made it a point of honour to be hospitable towards the son of the former owner, not without a display of the improvements he, Tam Drysdale, had brought about.

'Your father would not know the place again if he were to see it—eh, Mr. Mackinnon? You see there has been a considerable amount of capital invested both at the Haugh and the Hall, and capital can work wonders. These gates, now, cost hunders before they were out of the foundry. If you like to take a turn through the stables, or the cattle-sheds, or the green-houses, or to go over to the bleaching-ground and the dyeing-rooms, you'll see the extent of the improvements. But now, I mind, you were too young when you left to notice much ; however, you can guess.'

Beyond this courtesy and flourish of trumpets, Tam had not the slightest desire to go.

It came upon Tam with the shock of an unpleasant surprise he could hardly realize for scorn, and yet was forced to believe, with angry alarm, that this son of Gavin Mackinnon's—this officer lad without a penny, and with nothing but what appeared to Tam the fellow's cool superciliousness to sustain him—was having the impudence to make up to Clary. Nay, if the truth were to be told, it was rather Clary who, in a maidenly way, was having the folly to make up to him, distinguishing him by her notice, lending him every encouragement. Clary ! who was so proud, so wise, thought so much of herself, and looked so high.

The unpalatable idea thrust itself on Tam in the course of a dinner at Semple Barns.

Lady Semple did not draw the strict line between the old and the young, the married and the single, in the matter of dinners, which was the rule in Tam's circle. An invitation to dinner at Semple Barns was never limited to Mr. and Mrs. Drysdale. It always included Claribel; young Tam, if he could be had; even young Eppie sometimes, in spite of her not having come out elsewhere; and necessarily other young people to meet the young Drysdales.

Sir James's health was failing. He had been a shrewd old man, with a few foibles and testy finicalities which caused him to dismiss whatever trod on his toes as 'ridiklous, ridiklous.' He had really appreciated Tam Drysdale's broad common-sense and mother wit, and had enjoyed samples of them as a variety on the tone of the country gentlemen in the neighbourhood. But the host was no longer equal to protracted hospitalities. His guests knew it, and repaired in a body to the drawing-room within a quarter of an hour of the ladies quitting the table.

The elder men of the party had been confined to a neighbouring sheriff, who had far to drive, and started almost immediately; an old laird, who had little to say at any time, and had acquired a trick of falling asleep wherever he was; and Tam Drysdale. Sir James, on his part, conceived himself bound to devote whatever energy was left in him to the discomfited wife of the somnolent laird, who happened to be an old family friend.

Tam was by no means averse to the society of women, but he was not quite at home with Lady Semple and the Miss Vaughans, though he was one of her ladyship's first favourites, for whose good opinion she was anxious. In fact, the spare little woman in the plain silk gown, with the grey hair under her small lace cap, laid herself out for his entertainment, and aired all her theories, or what he called, in his

own mind, her fal-lals, in vain, for he still
fought shy of her. He could not speak to
his wife, content to sit with her hands in
her lap and be shown an album, which she
had seen twenty times before, by the more
disengaged of the Miss Vaughans. He
wished he were back at Drysdale Hall. He
did not think young Eppie and young Tam
had such a great loss in being absent, after
all. Auld Tam took to watching the young
people gathered round the piano, and speculating about them. Was he dreaming?
Could he trust his eyes that Clary was singing to that polished stick Mackinnon; that
she was looking to him to turn over her
music, pick up her handkerchief and get her
fan; that she was spending her strength in
putting a little animation into the listless
puppy?

There was nothing to find fault with in
the manner of the deed. Clary had been
well brought up, and was as modest as her
mother. Auld Tam knew there were girls

in the better classes who could not be depended on, but he thanked God he could
never have that to say of his daughters—
Eppie's daughters. Still, that would not
prevent Clary's ' throwing herself away like
a fool'—Clary who had been so wise—too
wise in the wisdom of the world, he had
sometimes been tempted to suspect. She
had always held her head high, and got a
great deal of her own way, so that it would
be hard to hold her in at this time of the
day. Tam began to doubt whether it was
not girls like Clary—self-sufficing, ambitious
—who astonished their friends by their in-
consistencies in the crowning acts of their
lives. It was as if the girl had professed
too much—as if nature, early trampled
down, rose up when it was least expected,
and revenged itself.

What did Lady Semple mean by not looking better after the young people committed
to her charge ? He recalled that Clary had
gone in to dinner with Mackinnon, and had

seemed well pleased with her partner. And
there was that lad of her ladyship's playing
at some game of making pictures, with one
of the English lasses, who was neither
bonnie nor braw, and looked old enough to
be his auntie; for all that, mischief might
come to one or other from the close association. She might mistake his intentions,
of which, doubtless, he had none to be mistaken; or he might be drawn into an en-
tanglement which would hamper him all the
days of his life. Why did Lady Semple
not mind the lads and lasses instead of
plaguing poor Sir Jeames to try the allot-
ment system, persuading herself she had
a knowledge of fat pigs, and pretending to
spin?

If this was all the good that was to
be got by Lady Semple's making such a
friend of Clary, auld Tam wished the girl
had never seen the woman. No, his fine-
looking, fine-mannered edicate lass, with
a fair fortune, was not daidlin', bletherin'

Gauvin Mackinnon's son's bargain, at any price.

Naturally Tam relieved his mind, whenever he was left alone with his wife, after their return, on the subject which had troubled him.

' Mother, you are more in the way of spying such ferlies than I am. Such troke is for you, and not for me. There is a great deal of forgathering [meeting] between the young folk here and at Semple Barns just now. There is no harm in that, but it may be carried ower far and have vexing consequences. I'm half ashamed to speak out— it seems a wrang to Clary; but do you not fancy she's leading on, without thinking, I dare say, that stupid, stuck-up chap of an offisher, Mackinnon? The couple are carrying on—in short, people will make remarks, and that must not be.'

In the beginning of this confidence Eppie blushed like a girl, her brown eyes twinkled, and her mouth pursed itself up with a mixture of importance and eager earnest.

'Have you seen something between them, father?' she asked, with a little excitement. 'I did think that Clary was different to him from what she was to the other lads. But it might have been fancy. I had aye telled myself Clary would not be easy to get round, or would be won by grandeur, and not give her heart a chance, which would have been a sore pity, for when a woman's heart is cauld, a's cauld. Now, he has little to say for himself, and is a kind of drifted aboot chield—ye ken what I mean, Tam—letting himself be mastered and carried awa' by circumstances; no like you, fechting every inch of the grund, and bund to come aff the conqueror. But I suppose it is all richt. You're strong enough for twa, and we've enough for everybody. Clary will ken her own mind, if anybody will, and you will not be hard upon them, if it come to that; you'll never stand in their way, and make two people—one of them your ain auldest dochter—meeserable ? To think of Clary with a hoose of her ain ! Only I'm thinking she'll not have a hoose, just rooms in the Barracks with the other sodgers' wives —well, to think of her following the drum may be stranger still. Eh ! it will be queer to have a dochter the length of being married. It will be little Eppie next, and it mak's you and me an auld couple, Tam,' she said, looking up at him with wistful eyes.

'Are you daft [mad], Eppie ?' cried Tam at last. 'Are you clean daft ? You may be auld, but you've your wisdom-teeth to cut yet. I tell you there is to be no word of sic havers. Mackinnon would be a most unsuitable man for Clary. I will not hear of sic folly.'

'But if they're in love, Tam ?' remonstrated Eppie, a little startled by his warmth, but still urging her plea as if it were irresistible. 'You would not cross true

love ! And as to his not being fit for her,
he's a very personable lad ; and though
he's a thocht canny, he'll be the easier
guided. Clary will take the reins wherever
she is ; she's made to rule. And have you
forgotten that his faither was the maister
here when you were the man ? There's a
sort of justice in another change of seats.
It will be a Mackinnon coming back to the
Haugh, as it was a Drysdale returning in
your shoon.'

'A fell odds in the return, and a very
limping kind of justice,' protested Tam
indignantly. 'Woman, you surely ken, if
onybody kens, that I wrocht for my return,
and earned it with the sweat o' my broo.
If a man's ain wife smoors [smothers]
his honour, I would not give muckle for't
at other hands. It was for a long time that
Gauvin Mackinnon continued the maister,
and me the man, and it would be the same
with this son of his—long he would hold
thegither ony sillar he might make out of

me! And it's that he's seeking when he seeks Clary,' the speaker declared bitterly. ' The men of the Mackinnons may be gude for little else nowadays, but they're gude arithmeticians when they mean marriage. It belongs to the kind.'

' Eh! that's not fair of you, Tam,' interrupted Eppie, scandalized. ' Clary's a bonnie, strapping lass—I've seen that he thocht sae in the laddie's een, mony a time, when he did not guess that I was so gleg [sharp]. You've no richt to belie him. But I did not mean to vex you,' added Eppie earnestly, quick to rue a sharp word to her husband. ' I never thocht of evening young Mackinnon to the like of you; but if he's Clary's fancy you would not pairt lovers.'

' Yes, I would,' maintained Tam doggedly; ' and for that matter, true love can take care of itself. But it is, as you say, a fancy, and nothing but a fancy, bred of idleset [idleness], and over-indulgence. Clary does not ken what she would be at,

and she does not ken what it is to live ; so
she makes sheep's-eyes at this jackanapes,
and she'll be the first to thank me for
saving her from him.　As for him, it's an
instinct of self-preservation—an easy way
of winning his living, say what you will of
what you've seen in his een.　Een have lied
ere now to women, and before their Maker.
So you'll take heed, and look after the twa ;
and let there be no more of this nonsense—
I will not have it !'

Eppie looked at him in silence, as he turned
away.　It was not for her to rise up in
open opposition to her husband, though she
could cross him firmly enough in the cause
of the bairns, and for conscience' sake.　Such
women as Eppie are always strong where
conscience is concerned.　She was her Tam's
wedded wife—his most loving wife to boot,
but she was not his slave.　However, in this
case, apart from the question of love, she did
not know that he was far wrong. She had
never really taken very kindly to the whether-

or-no lad of whom Clary approved, in spite of his good looks, and what some might hold his misfortunes. What she doubted was her ability to fulfil Tam's behest. She had even her suspicion of his unqualified power in this light, and she told him her opinion honestly, as a true wife should.

'You're a clever man, Tam Drysdale,' said Eppie, 'and you've focht your battle and triumphed; but you've never bridled or saddled hearts, or set bounds to the sea, that you should say you will not have this, or you forbid that, as if you were lord of all. And Clary is as high-headed as you are high-handed; she has it from you, and we've made her what she is. Will she mind me? Yes, she will so far; for she's a leddy, and so she cannot set her mither at nocht. And, of course, I can say, "You'll not have these Vaughan lassies and the lads in their train here soon again, Clary. I have never contered [contradicted] you about going to Leddy Semple's, but I

maun conter you now. Me and your
faither hold you're a thocht too often
there when Mr. Semple is at hame, and
Mr. Mackinnon is keeping him company.
And, on second thochts, Clary, I've given
up the idea of taking you all to the club-
ball. Your faither is not in the humour for
me going more out at present." Then she
would stare, and maybe she would argue a
bit, in a composed, half-laughing way, but
she would end by saying, "Very well,
mother; of course we'll not go if you don't
wish it." She would do nothing under-
hand, for I tell you Clary is a leddy—not a
make-believe leddy in fine clothes; she's a
leddy like Leddy Semple and the Miss
Vaughans. But would that be giving up
the lad? My certie! if you kenned
women, it would be mair like clinging to
him from that moment, through thick and
thin. It would not be as if she put her
arms round my neck, and grat [wept] on
my breast, as young Eppie might do, and

cried, "You and my faither ken best, mother, and I'll try and do your bidding; and if I fail, you'll try to forgive me." Na, na, Tam; you're strong, but you canna boo [bend] wills, and put out the dawn of love, like the lowe of a candle between your finger and your thoomb, to meet your views.'

Young Tam had gone little to Barley Riggs lately. Perhaps he felt he had enough to do without visiting—perhaps he had not forgiven Athole for dismissing him and his offerings from the hall of the house in St. Mungo's Square. Perhaps, with the perversity of human nature—one of the subtlest contradictions sinners have to strive against—he refused to give himself the comfort of Dr. Peter's hearty approval. He was shamefaced over what looked like a recantation of his diatribes against social inequalities. He shrank from reading the cool congratulation, the sly malice, the happy carelessness in Athole's bright eyes.

Dr. Peter and Athole talked of the young

man many a time, though she grew in-
voluntarily shyer of the subject than she
had been. Dr. Peter thought it as well to
leave young Tam to himself in these days
of struggling self-mastery; and Athole
began to fear the situation was changing
somehow, and that her grave and sardonic
companion, at older people's revels, would
be less himself, less comical in his youthful
disdain and disgust than of old. For
aught that she knew, he might begin to
talk 'shop' like the rest—the most zealously
of all, even as she had predicted that he
would live to become the keenest trader,
the most lavishly spending architect of
another Drysdale Hall. He might mellow
altogether, and wax brisk and lively. He
might seek to outrival Mr. Rowland in
story-telling, and herself in singing ' Major
Macpherson heaved a Sigh.' He might
ask her to dance a quadrille, or propose,
when the summer came again, to join Clary's
tennis-party; and the proceeding would be

as out of place as if Werther or Hamlet had executed the steps of a hornpipe, or suggested a game at battledoor and shuttle-cock. She could not say that she would like the transformation ; it would be a species of shock, and she grew absolutely apprehensive of it.

It was not at any dinner that Athole chanced to encounter young Tam for the first time after he was his father's partner. Neither was it on a charitable errand like that which had united them in the interest of the Miss Mackinnons. It was not at Drysdale Hall or Barley Riggs. The meet-ing took place amidst business surroundings. Athole had gone to the works one day with a little packet of patterns, and made her way to the pattern-room, to find the man at the head of the department, her usual referee, absent. There was another referee in his place, young Tam Drysdale, looming big and solemn, his very moustache showing portentously, seated at the man's desk, taking stock of the patterns, and qualifying himself for a pattern-furnisher.

Athole was herself again, to her own great satisfaction, in an instant, while young Tam, as he rose from his elevated seat, appeared undeniably confused and disturbed. Certainly she did not curtsey to him, but neither did she pay any heed to his overture to shake hands. She bowed sedately, and proceeded to do her errand at once. She unfolded her patterns, explained their designs, when these did not speak for themselves, asked his opinion of their merit, and whether he would have them, with the greatest propriety. She would have been a thousand times franker and more discursive to auld Tam.

When young Tam said of course, and that she was a better judge of such things than he was, she waved aside the simple truth with energy, as if it were the most fulsome compliment. The only approach she made to accepting the tribute, was

suddenly to overwhelm him with a disserta-
tion on patterns—so fluent, so thorough,
that it took away his breath, and did not
leave room for the introduction of a single
word on other topics. She dismissed herself in the middle of the harangue, with her
eyes sparkling, and at the same time a sort
of ' dare-to-come-with-me-to-the-door ' air,
that nailed the young man to the spot on
which he was standing.

But he was determined she should not
get the better of him here. He consulted
every available authority, drew elaborately,
with the help of a pair of compasses, a
calico pattern out of his head, as the fruit
of his investigations, and sent it over to
Barley Riggs, with a polite request that
Miss Murray would try something in this
style, which he had worked out, and should
like to introduce into the works.

Athole returned the pattern in a quarter
of an hour, with a civil note, proving in
half-a-dozen lines that most of the curves

were wrong, and mentioning that apparently colour had not come within the scope of the design.

When young Tam was initiating himself practically into the mysteries of the dye-vats, he had to wear a dyer's suit, and his hands—sometimes even his face—were a sight to contemplate. As a rule, he changed his dress and did his best to wash himself at the works; but once or twice—once by an accident which overthrew his arrangements, and twice when a spirit of boyish bravado came over him—he walked home in the guise which Tintoret may have displayed when he was still a lad about his father's dye-works, before he had taken up the palette and brushes of the prince of painters. In the dark December afternoon there was little light to distinguish what garb a man had donned. But at one point, where the road to the works joined the loaning which led to Barley Riggs, a lamp had been put up, and made a broad illumination in a circle, through which wayfarers had to go in passing the spot.

When young Tam, dressed in character, arrived at this stage of revelation on his homeward road, he was suddenly confronted by Athole Murray, who had strolled as far as the end of her own road to look out for her father returning from one of his medical rounds. Had young Tam got a glimpse of Athole a moment sooner, before he had himself entered the enchanted ring, which exposed all the horrible incongruity and fantasticalness of his coat—nay, his skin—of many colours, and if he could not have beaten a retreat down the path he had come up, in double-quick time, he would have been fool enough to risk his neck by attempting to scale, at a moment's notice, the high wall belonging to the works.

Now, had auld Tam been the victim, he would have advanced with the courage and composure of a wise man, though one side of his nose had been orange and the other blue, and there had been a splash of vermilion on his chin. It would have made no difference, though his age had been reduced to young Tam's, and it had been bonnie Eppie Mercer who had crossed his path when he was in this plight. His demeanour would have been much the same as it had been on the occasion of a little incident which had impressed his family. An enterprising mouse had invaded Drysdale Hall, penetrated to the dining-room, and actually ran up the foot of the master of the house, where he sat after dinner. There were screaming and scuttling on all sides. Young Eppie was on the top of the sideboard in as short a time as it takes to record the feat. Even Clary was moved to mount a chair. Mrs. Drysdale backed, in a hasty manner, from the table, drawing her skirts round her. Young Tam took up the poker. But auld Tam, with a robust superiority to all qualms of feeling, treated the aggressor simply as a 'fellow-mortal.' He sat where he was, gave his nether garments a shake, said in the easiest of tones, 'Get awa' with you, sir,' and went on with what he had been saying previous to the episode.

Though Athole Murray was plainly dressed, she was invariably neat, with a dainty neatness which is not always attained by the height of extravagance. She was particularly so this afternoon, as she stood in her dark serge, with the little thin, white muslin apron she was fond of wearing fluttering in the wind, and over her head and shoulders a quilted hood of old dove's-neck-coloured silk, which she put on when she visited her out-of-door pets.

'Mr. Thomas Drysdale as the clown in the pantomime, three weeks before Christmas,' she said, eyeing him from head to foot, taking in every daub and stain, and making the miserable man visibly conscious of the sum of them.

'The performance has one merit—it is gratis,' he said hurriedly; 'and if you will stand aside, Miss Murray, so that I may not get you into a mess, it won't be tedious.'

'Oh, I don't mind a stain or two,' she said, in the most obliging manner. 'I can always use salts of sorrel. I could recommend them honestly. But how did you get so many and such bright patches? Did any colour get on the cloth? You haven't tumbled into the vats?'

'No,' he answered shortly; 'but I'm a bungler—I always was, and always shall be; and there's an end of it. Will you let me pass, Miss Murray, without giving yourself the trouble and annoyance of becoming further acquainted with the beastly condition I am in?'

'Of course, but don't be hard upon yourself: indeed, you do not always bungle—you have done the thing completely this time,' she said, her eyes overflowing with laughter; 'the doubt is, will it pay?'

'It is no matter whether it pays or what it costs, if it ought to be done,' he retorted, with his old lofty manner, and the odd figure vanished in the darkness.

Athole went back to the house into the parlour, and stood looking into the fire. The fun passed out of her face, and was replaced by a wistful gravity. Her father found her thus, and she turned and said to him, without any preamble, as if she were announcing a discovery she had just made:

'Father, young Tam Drysdale is a fine fellow.'

'Have you only found that out now, Athole?' Dr. Peter replied, raising his eyebrows.

'Well, he hides his head under a bushel of extravagance,' she said, as an apology for her slowness; 'I suppose all modern heroes are laughable. The penalty of looking ridiculous is what they must suffer for their spice of heroism.　Don't you think there is a grain of heroism in a man —especially a young man's owning that he has been in the wrong, and eating his leek, so thoroughly as young Tam is doing ?'

'Yes; and what is more, it is heroism of the right, not the stagey, sort.　It is not particularly picturesque, and if it has a flavour of self-martyrdom about it, let us be thankful it is common homely self-martyrdom, not martyrdom on stilts.　The victim will not exalt himself over it.'

'It would be a good deal finer, as well as less absurd, if the hero did not make wry faces,' remarked Athole reflectively ; ' but one cannot have everything.'

It may have been by way of bringing about a hardly hoped-for perfection, and of serving as a wholesome discipline for young Tam in the interval, that Athole's pungent mockery flourished as much as ever, in their casual intercourse, after this date.

CHAPTER XVII.

THE COMMON TEMPTATION, WITH ITS USUAL ACCOMPANIMENT.

A PERIOD of remarkably flourishing trade followed in Glasgow. The recent prosperous years had all been leading up to this flush of enterprise and attainment. The expansion, if it did not pervade every source, reached to many departments of trade. Never had the hammers of the boiler-makers and the shipbuilders rung with more inspiring din, sending sonorous music down the misty river. Never had such strings of casks rumbled heavily in and out of the sugar warehouses and the spirit vaults. Never had St. Rollax and its sister chimneys vomited forth heavier volumes of tainted smoke. Never had the Exchange been so thronged and so busy, or Buchanan Street so crowded with promenaders and purchasers, or the Broomielaw so besieged with the shipping of all nations.

Mechanics and mill-hands had the maximum of wages. The homes of employés abounded not only in comforts, but in expensive, inappropriate luxuries—in port wine, oysters, and early strawberries; in rosewood couches, pianos, and featherbeds. The women of the class figured, on high days and holidays, in silk and lace. The custom of the smaller shops became steady and richly remunerative; that of the larger swelled enormously, till it reached so grand a scale of fortune-making that it ceased to be worth while asking the hitherto crucial question whether the process were wholesale or retail.

There seemed a limitless buoyance in the markets, an inexhaustible capacity for buying and selling beyond what had ever been dreamt of. Only invention, of which necessity is the parent, languished, and Dr. Peter, out at Barley Riggs, shook his head.

'It is a fever-fit,' he said to Athole, ' when the patient looks full in the face and rosy, with an eye like a star, and a pulse beating like the throbs of a steam-engine, and when the man has the strength of ten men. But even before the collapse, which will not tarry, can come, a train of evils, like Michael Scott's wee devils, will start into being, come to the front, and plague the man for work to do to employ their spare energies, till he is worn out with the very power that is about to quit him in a moment, and leave him next to dead on his bed.'

But what although there were fewer Glasgow patents taken out this year than for a dozen or more years before? What although words of warning were spoken in the country by an elderly poorish man who

had gone far and come back with his hands
not above a quarter full, so that he had to take
the not very distinguished post of doctor at
the Drysdale Haugh Works, and be thankful for it ?   This was a man who, as many
would have said, had ' made a mull ' of his
own life ; it signified little, and might be
taken as a matter of course, that he should
deliver a jeremiad on the uncertainty of
fortune.   All the big men, the great traders
and financiers, were taking the tide at its
height, and seizing the opportunity to extend their already vast operations, to double
and quadruple their huge receipts.   It
seemed as if the rebound would never reach
them.   This condition of splendid success
must be fortified and confirmed, until it
lasted to the extreme border of the century.

Men were so eager to avail themselves of
the chances opening out before them, that
wherever they had irons at all, they put
every one into the fire.   Speculators caught
at the materials out of which millions might

be made, and launched them on the rising
waters, with a faith that scarcely knew a
doubt. A large amount of capital was
lifted out of the old channels, which, by
comparison, paid miserably, and laid out in
the new cent. per cent. ventures of a brilliant
era in commerce. Credit followed capital,
and he was counted happiest who could
command most, who had a bank of which
he was one of the principal directors at
his back, into whose cash-box—speaking
figuratively—he could dip his hand at will;
or who belonged to an old-established firm
in high repute for sagacity and wealth; or
a new firm whose good fortune kept step
with its daring, so that it dazzled the eyes
of its contemporaries, forgetting to apply
the word 'plunging' to its great triumphant
undertakings.

The abounding life of manufacturing and
mercantile Glasgow was not confined to itself
by any means. It spread in wider and wider
circles, till it might be said to girdle the

world. The zone of trade extended from France to Russia, from the East to the West Indies, from America in the far north to America in the far south, from the territory of an enlightened Khedive in ancient Egypt, to the domains of a fore-seeing Queen in the special Pacific Island which had renounced cannibalism. In all these quarters men felt that great Glasgow was up and doing, that her craftsmen were wielding their brawny arms, and her merchants busying their shrewd brains with glorious results to the prosperity of lands beyond the seas.

Even the people who were least touched by the strong impetus, awoke to a distant rumour of the city's tremendous trans-actions and mighty profits, and invented fables more incredible still of the men who were puddlers, or winders, or dock-labourers to-day and princes to-morrow; of granite palaces which were equivalent to streets paved with gold. The risings in life at the Australian and American diggings were

a trifle to the upheavals in Glasgow society
—nothing was said at this moment of the
corresponding downfalls. The gold nuggets
of Ballarat and San Francisco were not to
be spoken of in a breath with the floating
capital of Glasgow—the real nuggets were
bills of lading and invoices. Tyre and
Ormus, in their traditions, must thence-
forth hide their diminished heads; Manchester bolstered up by Salford, and Liver-
pool backed by Birkenhead, had better withdraw from the idle competition.

Tam Drysdale was not out of the vortex,
though for a time he trod it cautiously, more
so than young Tam. When the latter en-
countered the full sweep of the current, he
lost his head a little, as he found the order-
books no longer fit to contain the orders and
commissions for calico of every tint and
pattern pouring in from the ends of the
earth. Indeed, the longest hours were not
long enough. All the workmen that could
be pressed into the service, though they

were to work day and night, would not have availed to bring the supply on a level with the demand. It was the first time that the young man had come into personal contact with the intoxication of trade, which was wont to address itself chiefly to the middle-aged, and to make up to them for the passing away of earlier stimulants in the visionary dreams of youth and the strong passions of manhood.

But, as time rolls on, the hurry of trade, in England and America particularly, engrosses younger and younger men, and becomes often their keenest pursuit. This is especially the case with the gilded youth of both countries. It had not been so hitherto with young Tam Drysdale; but it had been predicted of him, and who was he that he should resist the stream which was carrying all before it? What was characteristic about his plunge was that it took colouring from his previous associations. Young Tam, if left to himself, would have gone in a little wildly for ventures in his business, as the means of a millennium in trade, by an immediate raising of the masses, and rendering them decent and happy for ever afterwards, with civilization and Christianity borne in the conqueror's car from pole to pole.

Auld Tam knew better than that, but his blood was up at last, and then it became plain what a giant in his sphere the man was. How he could contrive, organize, and execute on the most colossal lines, till beside his achievements the greatest deeds of his neighbours grew dwarfed. His office and works, his branch of trade, Glasgow itself, felt proud of him, and the sweet incense of general homage to auld Tam, who in his boyhood had been the poorest artisan of them all, rose to his brain also. The self-approbation and vanity which had never been deficient in his composition waxed rampant and soared to sublime heights.

Tam's confidential talk became vapouring. He spoke as if every dyeing and calico-printing business in the world must yield to his and merge into it; as if all other trades would grow subordinate to the staining of cotton cloth in different colours and the stamping it in various designs; as if the wonders which chemical affinities and repulsions could produce had never been sounded to their depths, but he—Tam Drysdale—or if not he, his son, young Tam, was the man to sound them, and to discover the dye of dyes—before which Tyrian purple, Venetian green, Derby blue, magenta red, and coal-tar mauve, would sink into dimness and eclipse. He would witch the world with noble dyes. The kingdom of beauty should own his magnificent contributions. His grandsons would inherit the land when dyeing and printing had their proper place among the arts and sciences, and auld Tam's descendants were the princes of dyers and printers. It was hearing his father, wise on all else, discourse thus madly that cured young Tam of his own dawning delusions.

In truth, the strain of that period of over-trade was awful, and it spoke much for the strength and balance of those West-country minds, that they were only shaken —not crushed and overthrown for ever— by the fierce tension. As the race quickened to lightning-speed, a tendency to push production to impossibilities in fair trade, to substitute spurious for genuine articles, to flood the markets with inferior goods, and pander to the craving for cheapness by apparent underselling, became more and more conspicuous. Auld Tam did not fall into this snare; he was at once too clear-sighted and too honest. But the necessity of fighting with his own weapons against such rivals, and the determination to come off the victor, drew him farther and farther into lawful but perilous speculation.

Commensurate with the strain was the exhaustion of such times. Men must have relaxation, and they must have artificial support, else flesh and blood would not endure the ordeal to which they were subjected. Different classes of men and different men themselves took their sops in various ways. The New-Year time, according to old style, was kept with such bestial excess, riot, and waste, by many of the people, as dismayed their best friends. Who was to know that the finer spirits, coming between the scum and the dregs, took their pleasure temperately, soberly? The select few among the working-men were laying by for an independent, peaceful old age, were rising in the social scale, carefully cultivating tastes for higher, more exquisite pleasures, making time for attendance at schools and lectures, buying books and reading them, haunting museums and picture-galleries. With the first breath of spring these men would snatch sails 'down the water,' and runs into the country; would nourish grand projects of holiday excursions

to Ireland, to London—that capital of the
world; to Manchester, or Birmingham—
Glasgow's sister town; to France, or Bel-
gium—wide flights after the old yearly
trips to Arran and Largs, with which the
able-bodied holiday-makers had been for-
merly satisfied.

It would seem as if the mode of living
all over Glasgow altered at this time, and
the rate of family expenditure increased in
proportion. Men who were in their shops
and offices late and early, who were pursued
by letters and caught by telegrams, whatever
the season—on the wedding-morning of this
lad, and when that father's first-born lay
cold in death—who were, in fact, hunted
like runaway slaves to the last gasp, had
need of all the indulgences and all the
support which money, dearly earned, could
procure for them. If their weakness should
dream of haunches of venison, pipes of red
Burgundy, whitebait soaked in white wine,
let the spent toilers have their desires,

though they had been contented at no distant day with legs of mutton, cod's head and shoulders, poorish claret or sherry, and the native vintage of the country. When the over-burdened men returned home in the small hours, and sought to sup on devilled turkey, pine-apple, and the last best brand of champagne, don't deny the wearied wights what they sought, though the least surfeit might increase the danger of apoplexy; it was to be hoped that lemon-squash and a pick-me-up would restore the balance next morning.

If wives and daughters, mothers and sisters, never saw their mankind from the drab-coloured dawn to the mirk midnight, except on Sundays; if even then the men were engrossed and oppressed, slept like logs in and out of the churches—to which Glasgow never neglects to go—and when awakened were flighty and cross beyond the conception of the liveliest imagination, surely the women, in their turn, deserved compensation for their enforced loneliness and dulness, in the loss of rational intercourse with the heads of their houses, Give matron and maiden their share of the spoil, which was costing everybody dear, in cookery and confectionery, to suit feminine tastes, in bigger houses, finer furniture, more servants, in sables and sealskins, Duchesse and Valenciennes lace, in jewel-cases, opera-boxes, and carriages— where carriages had never been hinted at before. The two turning-points fondly contemplated in many a Glasgow career— 'to be riding in a carriage, and to be keeping a butler'—were attained by a multitude this year. By the way, this riding in a carriage seems peculiarly the goal of West-country ambition; nowhere else do men and women, who have stood behind a counter, toiled in shirt-sleeves, washed at a washing-tub, take instantly and inevitably to private carriages, like ducks to water, as the inhabitants of St. Mungo's city take to

them. And after the carriages, but at a
considerable distance, come the large yachts.

When all was done, it was no great entertainment to be luxurious and splendid *en
famille*. More and more visiting had to be
resorted to, in order to put the top-stone to
the fairy edifice, to divert the thoughts, to
rouse the imagination, to excite the languid
senses. When there was a moment to spare,
it was filled up by some dinner or evening
engagement. There was the theatre, if
there was nothing else. The Glasgow
clubs were becoming more and more like
the London clubs; the whist-play was excellent, and if whist formed too strong meat,
there were Napoleon and *vingt-et-un*. But
the theatre was still the *pièce de résistance*.
Glasgow could afford to pay the lessee to
bring down the greatest stars to strut and
sing and charm away its idle moments,
when idleness there was none, unless among
the women. There was not even the most
necessary repose. The hurry of life was

becoming hotter, more entangling and be-
wildering. The pace grew terrific. 'I
wish I could get a breathing-space to scart
my broo [scratch my brow], no to speak of
saying a prayer!' exclaimed an unhappy
man on the verge of desperation.

There were other men and women who
had long ago ridden in their carriages and
kept their butlers: these thrice fortunate
individuals bought more of the estates
which the old country gentry saw themselves compelled to bring to the hammer;
rented the best deer-forests; extended
and enlarged ranges of conservatories and
picture-galleries; had visions of entering
Parliament, or going on the turf—if only the
men had leisure. Fathers promised their
elder sons and daughters trips up the Nile
and voyages round the world, and sent
their younger children to the most strictly
select and outrageously expensive schools.
that could be heard of for love or money.

Still, as the ball went round merrily,

while handsomer incomes were taken for granted, and larger sums spent simply as a matter of course, there appeared the more absolute necessity for unrelaxing exertions to maintain the great trade which was to feed all these drains. The daughters of the horse-leech were crying, 'Give, give!' and refusing to add 'Enough.'

The readers of Tennyson's 'Palace of Art' know that there is only one end to self-indulgence, of however high a kind. The appetite fails, the food palls, the mind turns and preys upon itself, or it demands coarser and more powerful fare, and fierier stimulants. Men and women in all grades, who had been modest, contented, domestic, temperate, before the period of inordinate activity and prosperity, received from it the fatal bias which left them, after long years perhaps, arrogant, dissatisfied, unable to remain quietly at home, gluttons, drunkards in secret or openly.

At the same time, it would be false to say

that the season of success was put to no
great end. Grand improvements were in-
augurated and brought to pass, worthy the
public spirit of the mediæval Italian cities.
Magnificent acts of charity, which the middle
ages hardly knew, were performed without
a grudge, almost without an effort. The
citizens of St. Mungo's city seldom button
up their pockets. Her big, burly merchants
are very humane, whatever their faults.
Many of them are as liberal-hearted and
open-handed as any men in Christendom,
dispensing their bounty without hesitation or
fuss. There is a gruff 'Say no more about
it' tone in their generosity, which has a
curious delicacy in its very abruptness.
The fellow-feeling among the inhabitants
is strong. In order to buy fresh machinery
for a burnt-out or sold-out manufacturer, or
to furnish the means of independence to the
helpless, destitute children of a former
townsman, five thousand—ten thousand—
pounds have been subscribed for within

an hour on the Exchange, with no stipulation made, except that the names of the donors should be withheld, in order that the recipients of the gift might remain in ignorance of their benefactors.

The almsgiving at this date was lavish, like everything else; and Tam Drysdale had his hand in it, as well as in sending to London for lists of dinner-services in silver-gilt, and for having out a famous authority to Drysdale Hall to see whether the corridor could not be supplied with panels painted in fresco by all the first artists in Europe. In the face of such prodigality auld Tam still raised a storm in the house when he found a crust of bread had been thrown to the pigs, and threatened to discharge a groom because he had paid a few pence beyond the ordinary charge for the feed of a horse in a country-inn stable. And all the time there was a pauper lunatic out at Gartnavel who clawed at the door of his cell, and chattered of Mackinnon of Drysdale Haugh.

CHAPTER XVIII.

DR. PETER AND ATHOLE MURRAY MAKE THEIR STAND.

An elderly man with his young daughter, living in full sound of the periodical revolution in Glasgow habits and manners, did not follow suit. Life at Barley Riggs went on exactly as it had done before these busy, delirious days. Not a change did the family make in their routine, for they had still plenty of time for everything. Not a fresh incongruous article was added to the old simple seasoned household gods. Athole had not an additional gown of costlier material. Dr. Peter even bought fewer books than usual, and denied himself an improved telescope which he had thought

of buying. He could do star-gazing without it, every time he was called out on a
clear night, and perhaps it was not worth
the while of a man of his age to fix the
study on the latest scientific basis. It
seemed as if the family were called upon
to testify to a different order of things, and
to utter their small protest against the
opposite extreme.

The only one who murmured was the
handmaiden Jeannie. For she would come
and lay siege to Athole with tales of the
dainties and 'bonny-dies' [pretty things],
the cakes and puddings, the trays and
mirrors, which were now to be seen in the
houses of the Haugh work-people, as plenti-
ful as blackberries. Jeannie appeared to
feel it as a personal injury that the table at
Barley Riggs was not more richly furnished,
but was kept as wholesomely plain and
light in its good and sufficient cookery as
ever; and that her young mistress would
not launch into the attire of an extravagant

countess, in order to afford Jeannie a pre-
cedent for doing likewise within her sphere.
The maiden was not very wise, but she was
a kindly-disposed girl, knew a good place
when she had it, and, though she was
restive, retained a creditable respect and
regard for the master and mistress who
had taken a constant interest in her wel-
fare.

There were many more than Jeannie,
among people who ought to have known
better, who thought it very absurd that the
household at Barley Riggs should be standing still while the rest of the world was
advancing. These judges viewed with loud
scorn the old-fashioned, poor-spirited, unneighbourly pair. Yes, Dr. Peter and
Athole, who in their corner, with their
stinted means, kept abreast of much of
the thought of the day, were called old-
fashioned, and the man and woman who
had entered the breach to deliver the
Miss Mackinnons, were styled poor-spirited

and unneighbourly. To row against the stream is not only hard work—it strikes the mass as an ungracious performance.

Certainly Dr. Peter's income did not vary much with the rise of the popular funds. He did not take the money he had saved out of the old investment, in order to put it into the new, and quadruple the interest. Tam Drysdale had proposed that the men with their higher wages should contribute a larger moiety, as he himself agreed to do from his increased profits, to their doctor's pay. The men were willing, but Dr. Peter interfered, and limited the addition to the lowest sum. He said the working world would have need of all their spare pennies when the rate of orders and wages had fallen again, as it was bound to subside. He had no more doubt of slack times coming round, in a kind of natural order, than that cloudy strata would follow upon tracts of blue sky, and the east wind succeed the west. Most people agreed with him in theory, but in practice he was thought a Jeremiah for his pains.

There was a peculiar element of coolness and repose about Barley Riggs at this time, in contrast to the fever and unrest in its vicinity. Yet life was not without its excitement there, as elsewhere. Dr. Peter had specially interesting cases and problems which engrossed him. Athole hit on a new pattern, or was inspired with a design beyond the range of calico-printing, which she burned to express in wood or on earthenware, and managed to work out in a halting manner that did not render the idea barren, but by the very difficulty of clothing it in material form, made it fruitful in amended ideals, if in nothing else. All the news of all the world, ancient and modern, came to them in books and journals which the couple could study, digest, talk of in earnest and in jest, for Dr. Peter and Athole were great and good talkers together.

The seasons were constantly bringing some new thing—the first snowdrop, the catkin on the willow, the blossom on the geau-tree, the earliest rose, the latest hazel-nut. Dr. Peter and Athole, though the latter in a less degree—for the young are too full of the mystery of themselves to be always open to nature—scarcely ever missed a fine sunset, the evening star hanging tremulous in a daffodil sky, or the full moon when she was riding without check, white and glittering, in the purple dark-ness beyond her track. The two rarely lost the look of the garden before the morning sun had melted the cranreuch on bough and leaf; or that other aspect when spring had come, and the earth was brown, with the grass springing, the reddened buds swelling, the softest haze of genial mist hovering over the tender, everlasting youth of the scene.

There was never a day or an hour when some event did not happen in the animal kingdom at Barley Riggs, and it never happened without observation and interest —another calf, another kid, a brood of spring chickens; the patriarchal dog held fast in a rabbit-trap, the baby kitten catching a mouse; this bird beginning to sing, that to moult; Dr. Peter's pony undergoing a clipping, Athole's old Shetland treated for a cough; the first butterfly, the first swallow.

Early morning hours were kept at Barley Riggs, though Dr. Peter had not to bolt his breakfast and start for Glasgow by the nine o'clock train. On the contrary, he rose not later than seven, and—unless it were raining pigs and whistles—took a stroll over the place to see that all was right, leant a minute over the gate to have a 'crack' with this or that familiar working man or woman who had been home for breakfast. Or he made a bolt out to inquire for some patient who might have had a restless night and be wearying to see his doctor, for Athole did not approve, if the obligation were not urgent, of her father's attending his sick before he had broken his fast. Then Dr. Peter walked back to the house as fresh as a daisy, and ate his meal in a leisurely, sensible fashion.

He hailed the postman, read his letters, glanced over the newspaper, and cleaned and fed such furred and feathered retainers as fell to his care. Next he changed his coat, and set out on his morning round, leaving Athole and her handmaiden to the household cares which belonged to the early part of the day, and were as regularly and satisfactorily discharged on their part as another mission was fulfilled on his.

Dr. Peter practised what he preached. He recommended early dining as the rule of life for working-men and invalids alike, and he came home in anticipation of his dinner an hour after noon, and did a little work in the surgery—the constant accompaniment of a country doctor's house, where he was training a homely assistant, whose college terms were yet to begin. In addition to this assistant, Dr. Peter had the services of a stout boy for his pony and in the garden, and on him the doctor bestowed a few additional minutes of his time before he appeared in the parlour at the sound of the dinner-bell.

There was a smoking season after dinner, when the great advantages of a veranda which had been erected on one side of the house were regularly recognised. Athole was generally with Dr. Peter then—'playing,' as he called it, taking her part in a lively argument, teasing or being teased, hearing and giving the gossip of the morning.

A little later the two frequently walked out together when he had such professional visits as he could pay in this way, or he took another round to keep his evening clear, or he worked in the garden. In the latter case he would call to Athole where

she sat at work in the window, every ten
minutes or so, to come out and listen to
some weighty piece of information he had to
give her—on the state of the mould, which
would require special treatment; about a
singular grub he had turned up; with regard
to the flight of the rooks, which determined
the next day's weather; or the appearance
of the gooseberry-blossom as a criterion of
next July's crop of gooseberries. If the
weather were hot, and he felt tired, Dr.
Peter would withdraw to the old Dutch
summer-house, in which he remembered his
young brothers holding merry smoking-
parties, and read or meditate, or take a
nap, as the humour moved him.

In winter Dr. Peter would be more in
his surgery, or he would retire to the loft
in which he did his joinery and turning,
when Athole would look in upon him, and
put a summary stop to his working more
than he was able.

At the tea-table—set out in the old

methodical substantial fashion, with Cowper's
' hissing urn ' in the place of honour—Dr.
Peter came out in full force. He was as
fond of tea as if he had been Dr. Samuel
Johnson, or an old washerwoman, he was
accustomed to say. He insisted if people
would drink the beverage rationally, well
' wafted ' with bread, or perhaps a slice of
tongue or corned beef, or ewe-milk cheese,
he would stake his credit as a medical man
that it would not do the veriest old wife
harm. It was the unnatural, senseless
' babbling ' at the drink at all hours of
the day which played the mischief. At
the same time he regarded the meal as
essentially feminine, the woman's hour, to
which, if you would cultivate her good
graces, you must do justice by rendering
yourself as agreeable as it was in your power
to be. He thought no woman ever looked
better than when she was presiding at a
tea-table, and dispensing her own peculiar
good things. He liked to see Athole in

his sister's place; his wife, whom he had married and immediately taken abroad, where' she died, had never been at Barley Riggs.

Dr. Peter generally revealed at the tea-table what book he had unearthed from his shelves, or intercepted at the railway station, and deposited in his pocket to surprise Athole. 'Ah ha, lassie! you do not know what I have got here,' he would cry in glee, patting the bulging-out pocket. And Athole would guess wildly, wide of the mark, till she grew impatient. Then he would give up his treasure, and she would handle it, peep into it, read sentences from it like a connoisseur. She would hurry to get her work, when he would read to her till his eyes were weary, and she would take her turn and read to him, with plenty of pauses for comment, contradiction, or agreement.

If the book were either not interesting enough, or too interesting, he would call a halt, and bid Athole sing to him, which she did pleasantly enough, either with or without the piano. She had a gift for quaint 'genteel comedies' and farces, for old songs like 'Major Macpherson heaved a sigh,' '*Monsieur, je vous n'entend pas,*' 'My face is my fortune;' though she could not give 'Logie o' Buchan,' or 'Wha's at the window, wha, wha?' with such naïve sweetness as young Eppie Drysdale rendered them.

If there was anything left of the evening, Dr. Peter would challenge his daughter to draughts or bézique, and whoever the victor was, he or she was rarely great enough to refrain from crowing over the vanquished.

The master of the house was a country doctor, and suffered in full from the lingering dilatoriness and sudden panic which causes the poorer, more ignorant country people to try every remedy in illness save sending for the qualified judge, and to

practise the patience of Job till the small
hours, then to rush helter-skelter, disturbing
the lieges generally, and knocking an unhappy man out of his hard-earned bed, for
help which he might have bestowed with
comparatively little trouble, and to more
purpose, half-a-dozen hours before.   Still,
Dr. Peter could generally manage to keep his
hours sufficiently regulated for him to act as
family priest.   He could appear with his
household for a brief time in what he
believed to be the Great Presence, acknowledge an Almighty Father's supremacy, and
supplicate His mercy.

Sometimes patients were so thriving and
considerate as to permit their doctor to eat
in peace his simple supper of a haddock or
a herring, or 'a shape of potted head,' and
drink the single glass of toddy which was
supposed to fortify him against the effects of
exposure and fatigue, if he were summoned
late, which occurred sufficiently often to
have tried the constitution, mental and

bodily, of a much younger man. Then Dr. Peter would rise and stretch himself, cry cheerily :

‘ Hey for boot and horse, lads,’ charge Athole not to sit up herself, or let Jeannie sit up for him, and go his way, perhaps not to be back till daybreak.

Sunday could not, in the nature of things, absolve Dr. Peter from the duties of his profession, since men sicken and die on the Saturday and Sunday indiscriminately. But, taken in their highest sense, these duties fitted in well with the day of Him who, on the Jewish Sabbath, restored the withered hand, and bade the palsied man take up his bed and walk. They rarely prevented Dr. Peter from going with Athole to join his neighbours in public worship, in the church where he held the office of an elder, the minister of which was one of his oldest and most esteemed friends. In other respects, Sunday was a day of rest to Dr. Peter, in the sense of a day quiet, and calm, and bright—for knitting closer family ties, for still more intimate association with nature, for reading his best books, for remembering friends near and far away, for communing with the unseen, and penetrating behind the veil.

Not only was Dr. Peter well content with these unhurrying days, as a leisurely end to an active career, a slight experience of the land of Beulah before he passed beyond the light of sun and star; Athole had the feeling and taste to be sensible of their fine flavour. She said to herself, truly, that she would not change her father and their home-life together for any other father—however well endowed and indulgent; or any other life—however full of change and movement. This was in spite of the fact that Athole's heart was 'hot and restless,' like other young hearts, that she felt tempted to welcome variety, emulation, opposition, so that it promised excitement, to be in the thick of the conflict, the rush of

the strife—of a good deal that was going on
in St. Mungo's city at this moment. She
could even have welcomed a passage at
arms with young Tam Drysdale, to strike a
spark from the steel. But always, when
Athole came to think of it, she grew sorry
for such a mood. She knew she was
wronging herself and her father, and wished,
in an exalted mood, that nothing at Barley
Riggs might ever alter, for nothing on earth
could be better.

Barley Riggs was not out of the range of
visiting and visitors, while Dr. Peter was
hospitable with all the friendly hospitality of
a man who has lived at a foreign station, and
known what a neighbour may be at a pinch.
But though he put his best before his
guests, it must be his natural best, what
was in keeping with his position and habits,
and only outran in a cordial, gracious way
his ordinary experience. From the first
day that Dr. Peter returned to Barley Riggs
and settled there, he set his face steadfastly

against display and competition for the prize in extravagant outlay, or in *recherché* attainment, the sole virtue of which was that it happened to be *recherché*.

'Our friends know what to expect from us, Athie,' Dr. Peter would counsel his daughter; 'and upon my soul I believe they will be better pleased with that than with something out of all bounds. If they're not, I am mistaken in them, that is all; and they had better stay away, and go where they can be served according to their fancy.'

'In what way?' inquired Athole tentatively.

'In what way? When a man looks round on crystal, silver, and flowers enough to dazzle and bewilder him, and reads a *menu* as long as his arm, containing three times as many dishes as he can touch.'

'There is no great harm in that,' said Athole mischievously.

'Wait. He eats what he is not accus-

tomed to ; what, very likely, is not good for
him, and what his instincts are often sound
enough to warn him away from, if he would
attend to them.   But no, he must ape his
neighbours, pretend to tastes he never felt,
and bolster up his gastronomical feats by
drinking less or more of all the wines and
liqueurs that are handed round, and pretending to like them, too, till he is miserable.
And if he does come to feel the liking he
has feigned, the worse for him.'

'Father, I am afraid you are talking
shop,' objected Dr. Peter's daughter. 'You
ought to have thrown the substance of that
speech into a paper for the *Lancet.*'

'Don't talk nonsense, child. We could
not afford such dinners, Athole, and we will
not try.   People have enough of that kind
of thing elsewhere. When they come to
us they must come for more than the bill of
fare, or for such a bill of fare as is perfectly
good and appetizing—even tasty of its
kind.'

'Now you overwhelm me,' professed
Athole.

'Lassie, what would the soldiers in ˈthe
Crimea, or in Zululand, or in Egypt have
thought of it ?   Yet it has not cost what is
equivalent to a poor man's house-rent for a
year, and will not spoil anybody's diges-
tion, or ruin me, though I were to give a
dinner to a dozen friends once a month.'

To the credit of mankind, no less than of
Dr. Peter and his housekeeper, when he did
indulge in giving unpretending, well-cooked
dinners, they were highly popular with rich
and poor alike.   Their success might be
due, in a degree, to his excellent qualities
as a host, and his gifts as a *raconteur*, and
to the able manner in which Athole abetted
him in both these directions. Yet it seemed
as if, in the leap which the west had taken
in wealth and luxury, there was a little less
relish for the mother-wit of the past, a little
less inclination to be reminded of ancient
thrift or waste, stoic endurance, or passion-

ate assertion. The present, the crowded
present, threatened to become all in all.
But to Dr. Peter the old records and stories
never lost their charm. He delighted in
picturing Glasgow when Queen Mary was
said to have given its name to a certain
suburb, then a country village, as she looked
at the crucifix in the palm of her hand, and
swore, in defiance of the rebel army barring
her way, ' By the cross in my loof, I will
sleep in Dumbarton this night !' He had
equal pleasure in recalling later centuries,
when golf was still played on Glasgow
Green, and a walk round it before breakfast
was the ' constitutional ' of all the active old
gentlemen in the town. He would fain
have known the ingredients of that hot
herb ale which the pedestrians afterwards
drank, with such relish and benefit, in
Currie's Close.

Dr. Peter fairly angered auld Tam by
speculating on whether he (Dr. Peter) would
not have liked Glasgow better when fish

was her sole trade, and Clyde's banks were
bonnie and blooming, and the air caller and
sweeter from Hamilton to Campbelton;
when the inhabitants of St. Mungo's city
thought nothing fairer or grander than
their own cathedral, beneath which good
Kentigern slept; when a double rainbow
spanning the Clyde, or a troop of 'merry
dancers' in the northern sky, was an event
worthy of notice, spoken of for days, no
more eclipsed and obscured by the rushing,
noisy obligations of trade, than by the reek
of a forest of chimneys which did not yet
exist.

CHAPTER XIX.

GLASGOW is not the most aristocratic city in
her Majesty's dominions. Her merchant
princes may be lavish of that wealth which
commands so much; their establishments,
both in town and country, may have passed
beyond the stage of soulless luxury and
sumptuousness, and attained the higher
distinction of intellectual culture. The
West-End clubs may be exclusive; the
city may have resources within herself,
which do something to counterbalance the
disadvantages of enormous traffic. Glasgow society, hospitable in every walk, may,

in the upper classes, be only too flatteringly kind to sprigs of gentility. For some of them do find their way to a field where they receive so much favour—condescend to bask in its sunshine, and profit by its substantial benefits. Witness the Miss Vaughans, Lady Semple's cousins, who were not disinclined to consider overtures of alliance, backed by full purses, from the sons of commerce. Still, as a matter of fact, Glasgow is not the haunt of the nobility and gentry of the United Kingdom. Titles, except in the case of Lord Provosts, or of titled men and women appearing at civic feasts, election and volunteer balls, or charitable breakfasts, rarely figure in the lists of company at this or that table.

For a real live baronet of ancient line and good estates, one who was neither a blackleg nor a prodigal, to alight and abide for any length of time—not merely to be passing a night in one of the best hotels, on his way to the Highlands—was for a *rara avis* to show himself, when a flutter of wings from all the common birds called attention to the fact. If the baronet happened to be young, and a bachelor, the flutter, which was always better defined in feminine quarters, became twenty times more eager and animated. The excitement referred to an event which did not happen often, but had been known to occur, and to produce the most charming consequences. Daughters of St. Mungo's city, like the daughters of Augsburg of old, had departed ere now with their tochers, to gild afresh old titles, to appear no more in commercial circles, but to be heard of from afar as denizens of the politest regions.

Public feeling pointed in this direction when the news spread abroad that young Horsburgh—of ' Horsburgh and Tennant,' the great West Indian merchants—who had been to Cambridge, had brought back with him for his Easter holidays his college chum, Sir Hugo Willoughby, of Willoughby

Court.   Sir Hugo was reported young,
handsome, intelligent, agreeable, of a race
dating from the Conquest—which is a great
deal better than dating from Adam—with a
rental that, though it did not come within
a tenth or twentieth part of the profits of
some of the larger city firms, was perhaps
safer, and was certainly not to be despised.
In addition, the rental was said to be accompanied by such a perfect old Court in
Lincolnshire, that the mere possession of it
conferred the finest odours of gentility on
its fortunate owner.

Moreover, Sir Hugo was likely to remain
for a time.   He was understood to have a
laudable curiosity about city life and trade
centres.   He would not only inspect warehouses, he would ride to cover with the
Lanarkshire hunting men ; he might take
a run in Guy Horsburgh's yacht.   Early
as the season was, he would be seen at the
dinners and balls of the select traders who
could claim the acquaintance of the family

in which Sir Hugo was staying. And, as if to render the public good greater, and the chances of war fairer for all, Guy Horsburgh had no unmarried sisters. There was no dangerous propinquity settling the question at once, and leaving hardly the ghost of an opportunity for any other girl.

Is it wonderful that the maiden heart of richest Glasgow heaved high, like the breast of Major Macpherson in the song, that many a council of war was held between mothers and daughters and sisters, this windy March, and many a box from court milliners in London, and even from Worth in Paris, was hastily conjured up with materials for the short but what might be the momentous campaign ?

Really, Sir Hugo was worthy of it on his own individual merits. He was a fine young fellow. The foundation of his principles had been laid by a good mother—a widow who had never ceased to mourn for the husband of her youth, whose son, her

only child, was the apple of her eye. From
her he had derived a remarkable amount of
ingenuousness and a dash of enthusiasm,
which such intercourse with the world as
he had commanded had failed to extinguish.
He was regarded as something of a young
Quixote at his University, which had been
his world for the most part, but he had possessed wit to defend his views. He was
manly, rather rash, and a little thoughtless;
but in his very thoughtlessness he was generous and honest—a lad to be liked first and
trusted afterwards. He was unconventional
—reckoning according to the last, the Eneas
Mackinnon, pattern of young men.

Sir Hugo had sufficient brains to seek to
extend his knowledge of humanity. It was
true that he had come to Glasgow with an ardent desire to learn all he could pick up about
one of the wonderful man-hives of Britain
and the world, as unlike as possible in its
ceaseless stir among all classes, and recur-
ring flights and falls, to the traditions of his

order. These pointed to dignified quiet and leisure, an established order of things, a God-appointed institution of rulers and ruled, of different sorts and conditions of men, who were to govern and obey, to amuse themselves and to work, to be helpful to each other while they remained far apart—above all, to rest content with the very different lots which Providence had assigned to them.

It is impossible to deny another motive which had brought Sir Hugo to Glasgow. He was young, and therefore merry, facile, and so open to temptation. He had heard amazing and unsurpassable stories of the incongruities and absurdities of Glasgow life, as of life at the diggings, of the gulf between the *nouveaux riches* and their former habits, and the blunders these lucky men and women committed. He was fain to test for himself the truth or falsehood of these travellers' tales, to have his share of the laugh that was habitually playing round the

comedy, in the better-informed world. But
his native generosity caused him to repent
of the deed before it was committed ; and if
he should see the slightest reason to qualify
his impressions, he would be the first to re-
nounce them.

As it chanced, Sir Hugo was delighted
with Glasgow life. Its powerful vitality,
innumerable lights and shades, and the mag-
nitude of its achievements, took hold of his
large stock of sympathy, and made a mark
on what was at this time his rampant imagination. He was quite capable of going
out of himself and his order to appreciate
qualities and conditions which, however
admirable in themselves, were foreign to
his earlier experience. Indeed, the novelty
of the situation was one of its chief attractions.

Young Horsburgh was not without *amor
patriæ*. He had been a good deal aggrieved
by the estimation in which he had found his
native city held in other regions, and by the

chaffing which he had been called on to
endure on its account.   One of his purposes
in bringing Sir Hugo down with him had
been to open his eyes, by showing him what
St. Mungo's city really was, and by proving
that there were not only as wealthy citizens,
but as good men and educated gentlemen
within its bounds, as were to be found in or
out of any city in Christendom.

Sir Hugo had not been a week in Glasgow
before his volunteered recantation out-
stripped the mark.   He out - Heroded
Herod, and went far ahead of Guy Horsburgh in his extravagant regard for Glasgow.   There was no enterprise like Glasgow enterprise ; there were no manufactures
like Glasgow manufactures ; no men and
women like those of Glasgow, wherever the
light of day shone.

It was only ordinary gratitude in Glasgow,
especially young Glasgow, to make an idol of
Sir Hugo in return, to say there never had
been a ' Prince Charming ' like him.   He

was so perfect a gentleman, so good-looking.
He was a little of a thread-paper as yet,
but that defect was mending daily since he
had attained his majority; besides, the slim-
ness stood out in agreeable relief to the
early tendency to heavy weights and large
outlines on the part of the city men.   And
nobody could refuse to grant that Sir Hugo's
clear olive skin, high nose, open forehead
and peaked chin became him exceedingly.
He was clever, pleasant, and high-bred.
In short, he had only one fault; he was
too easily pleased, too much inclined to be
everybody's body—so that his conquest, if
he were conquered in a special sense, would
argue rather a piece of good luck, a happy
accident, than a decided choice where he
was concerned, and a triumphant victory
for his conqueror.   But could there ever
be a smaller spot on the sun?

The commotion occasioned by the advent
of Sir Hugo Willoughby disturbed the equa-
nimity of even so self-controlled a young

lady as Claribel Drysdale. She was conscious of a wish to be introduced to the
stranger. She studied her toilet as other
Glasgow girls—competitors for his ready
smiles—studied theirs. She was gratified
by receiving his tribute of admiration. She
listened complacently to the little meaning
suggestions and half-veiled prophecies of
her friend, Lady Semple.

Her ladyship had suddenly developed
a capacity for match-making on Caribel's
account. It was a shame to her—Lady
Semple—the matron told herself, never to
have done anything of this kind on Claribel
Drysdale's behalf before. But then Lady
Semple knew that Claribel looked high,
while, on the other hand, it was not every
gentleman in her ladyship's circle who
would care to have Mr. and Mrs. Drysdale,
much as Lady Semple herself liked them in
their own place, for *beau père* and *belle mère.*
However, Sir Hugo was young, and good-
natured, and much in love with Glasgow

already, and Lady Semple did not think Lady Willoughby—the dowager in prospect —would make any serious objection, particularly as Claribel Drysdale ought to have quite a handsome fortune, and was in all respects decidedly presentable. Lady Willoughby was too kind and reasonable, and too devoted to her son to form an insurmountable obstacle.

Of course Claribel would not have done for Dick, even if the Honourable Lilias had been out of the question, with the whole Drysdale clan, and all that was objectionable in their rusticity continually turning up. But it was a far cry to Willoughby Court; and if any of the Drysdales, except Claribel, ever found their way there, as certainly they ought to do at some time, seeing they were quite respectable people, it would simply be as birds of passage.

Yes, the match might do very well, though it would not in any circumstances have suited Dick, who had never thought of it.

It might be the very thing for Sir Hugo, who, from all Lady Semple could hear, was too impulsive and heedless. He would be all the better for a wife like Clary Drysdale to look after him. She would make him an excellent wife, of whom any man in any position might be proud; and Lady Semple would be very glad to help Claribel to such a position—it would be a graceful act. Her ladyship had found her young friend a great acquisition at Semple Barns. She was exceedingly sensible, and had wonderful powers of adaptation and *savoir faire.*

Lady Semple knew she was standing in her own light, for she would miss Claribel when she was gone; but no selfish consideration ought to be suffered to spoil a young girl's brilliant prospects. The Vaughan girls need not be disappointed, for it could not be expected that Sir Hugo would think of either of them. They were too old, had no beauty to signify, and no fortune, while

their style, which might weigh with city
men, was nothing to him.

Claribel Drysdale was proud and delicate-
minded. She made no unbecoming advances
to Sir Hugo. She vouchsafed him no
further encouragement than she allowed to
other men beyond the range of merchants
and manufacturers; but she consented to
meet him wherever he was to be met. She
smiled graciously on his acceptance of an
invitation to dine at Drysdale Hall, which
auld Tam, not to be outdone by his neighbours, had sent Sir Hugo after calling on
him. Clary's smile was in spite of the
consideration, which none of the family
realized as she comprehended it, that there
were halls and halls; that is to say, that
Drysdale Hall and Willoughby Court should
not be mentioned in the same breath.

In all this Claribel had lost sight of Eneas
Mackinnon. He had slipped out of her
thoughts, had been superseded by the
glamour surrounding another man, who

promised to fulfil the desire of the girl's
heart, the dream of her youth. Perhaps it
may be said, small blame to her for it, so
instantaneously, without any sign of resistance, did the Lieutenant acquiesce in her
decision, and withdraw from the faintest approach to competition with his well-endowed
rival. Only a shade more weariness in his
weary, handsome face, and the dying out of
a spark of hope—it had never been more
than a spark—in his hopeless, not unkindly
eyes, betokened any sense of a change in
her manner, and a change in the world to
him. But, after all, Claribel, with the exception of young Tam, was the least moved
of any in the house by the coming of Sir
Hugo.

Auld Tam had grown accustomed to 'Sir
Jeames' as a neighbour and friend; but a
fine young English baronet, said to be cousin
to an earl, was a guest deserving first-rate
entertainment at Drysdale Hall. It was
worth while showing to him its unapproach-

able advantages, and the best of everything which money—its master's earning—could procure for him. Therefore, Tam was exacting and disposed to be fussy about the feast. He interfered in the matter of the dinner, to the disgust of the trained cook and housekeeper who had been foisted on Mrs. Drysdale. He ordered and counter-ordered—sent out emissaries from Glasgow with the delicacies which were not in season, and then supplanted them by other messengers with more cates which would not go with the first. During the whole time, the man himself would have preferred green kail to turtle soup, and a 'kipped herring' to turbot. He changed the wines more than once, putting himself out and overturning the arrangement of his cellar. He fidgeted about the decanting and non-decanting of the bottles, their heating and cooling, with the necessity for keeping the different vintages distinct.

Mrs. Drysdale's fine temper was as nearly

ruffled as it could be. Tam might have
had a little consideration for her, she said to
herself. He might have thought the burden
of the dinner was on her, not on him ; that
it was trial enough for her to face more fine
folk, after she had grown accustomed to
‘ Sir Jeames ’ and Lady Semple, without
making her miserable beforehand. She did
not know what had come over Tam. He
had got his own way with young Tam, and
it was flying in the face of a kind Providence not to be content. She feared prosperity was wasting her Tam. She could
have found it in her heart to hate this Sir
Hughie—or whatever he might be called—
who caused so much trouble.

But the next moment auld Eppie was
sharing young Eppie’s joyous excitement
about the grand young Englishman. They
were deep in a happy consultation as to
what flowers the two could coax from the
head-gardener—almost as formidable a subordinate as Mrs. Wood—to adorn, according

to the women's pretty devices, not only the drawing-room and the dinner-table, but the picture-gallery, to which Tam always took his cherished guests before or after dinner, as the light suited. The two were like an elder and a younger sister as they ran about, for the bonnie, buxom matron was still light and active, disposing pots of ferns and azaleas, jonquils, hyacinths, and heaths, wherever the pair imagined pots could be set to advantage. If auld Tam could have seen his wife and daughter just then, all his small difficulties would have vanished, everything would have appeared right in a moment.

Young Eppie did not dispute the fiat which had originally come from Clary, that since she—Eppie—was not to be sent to school, she could not appear at dinner when there was company at Drysdale Hall till she had attained the mature age of eighteen. Eppie, like her mother, was a reasonable, submissive being, unless when her affections made her stand at bay. She was perfectly well pleased only to be seen in the drawing-room with the tea and coffee, where, she said, Sir James and Lady Semple would speak to her, and maybe Mr. Horsburgh and ' Captain Mackinnon,' for she had seen them before, with any of the other ladies and gentlemen she knew. But she did not expect to be introduced to Sir Hugo Willoughby, for Clary would want him to hand her cup and turn over her music; besides, if he were so very grand, she—Eppie—could not tell what to say to him; she would be frightened out of her wits.

Guy Horsburgh, knowing something of the host and his ways, made an appointment with Tam at his office, and asked him to drive out the two young men to Drysdale Hall in time to see the stables and offices, which were in Sir Hugo's line.

Naturally, Tam complied with excellent grace, and he had been enabled to discourse, *con amore*, on his outward possessions for

three-quarters of an hour before the gentlemen entered the house.

Sir Hugo had listened, admired, been interested, been bored, been tolerant, felt that
a great deal of trouble was being taken on
his account; and thought that Horsburgh
had brought it on them, for he himself hated
to give trouble. Sir Hugo wished that he
had not to suspect the old gentleman—Tam,
in his prime, seemed a veteran to the lad,
little over twenty—was not blowing his own
trumpet. But very likely his cattle and
so forth were his hobby. It was not only
soldiers and sailors, but men of every calling—tinkers and tailors, too, he dared say
—who delighted to turn Cincinnatus when
they got the opportunity. He supposed
farm-buildings and stables were in his line,
but he would rather have seen the dye-works;
only, if he had to be shown by demonstra-
tion that there were no such vats in the
country as the Drysdale Hall vats, and had
each appraised at its proper value—well, it

was a trifle tedious, begging the old gentleman's pardon, and he would not broach the
subject, but would hold everybody excused
for the omission.

CHAPTER XX.

'A YOUNG THING JUST COME FRAE HER MAMMY.'

As the party were approaching the main entrance, Tam, who was leading the van, caught a glimpse of an under-gardener, whom he judged to be the defaulter in some trifle amiss with the terrace that had just caught the master's orderly eye. Without ceremony, he turned aside to call the culprit to account. In the meantime, Guy Horsburgh saw young Tam, who had been over at the works, coming up the avenue, and waited to meet him. Sir Hugo, thinking the others were close at his heels, entered by the door which the servant had thrown open, and was shown by himself to the picture-gallery.

Sir Hugo was not alone. One of the daughters of the house, doubtless—though surely not the one he had seen before—had not gone to dress, and was bending over a flower-stand, and so intent upon shifting a pot that she did not notice anybody was there.

'Allow me, Miss Drysdale,' said Sir Hugo, who had too little self-consciousness to feel uncomfortable on his own account, advancing like the pink of courtesy that he was.

Young Eppie started, looked up with parted red lips, and dark eyes so wide open that the long curling lashes ceased to veil them. So far from having gone to dress, she had done nothing to repair the result of her work since luncheon. Her fringe—oh! she could not tell what state her fringe was in ; but she did not believe there was a hair that she had not pushed out of her eyes or

tucked behind her ears half-a-dozen times.
Her hands were green and red from contact
with the flower-pots. Her morning gown
was the oldest she possessed, and the one
which had received the worst usage; it was
dragged to one side because Eppie had just
trodden on the hem and torn a portion of the
skirt out of 'the gathers.' All this when
the 'Allow me, Miss Drysdale,' spoken by
an English tongue, confirmed, beyond the
possibility of mistake, the impression which
her single startled glance had at once conveyed. This strange young man, with his
horrible ease, was the very Sir Hugo
Willoughby for whom everybody had been
making such preparations. What would
Clary think! What would her father—nay,
what would her mother say, if they knew
the plight in which their chief guest had
found Eppie!

With a little half-stifled shriek of dismay
which she could not altogether repress,
Eppie, obeying the first impulse, turned and

fled like the wind to the nearest door. In
a moment she disappeared, as if no such
disordered young figure had disturbed the
propriety of the beautiful room. The only
relic she had left behind was the very vestige
which had remained of Cinderella—one little
slipper had dropped in the flight.

Sir Hugo stood amazed—amused. Was
this the behaviour of the young Glasgow
ladies when they were taken by surprise?
But, ye gods! what a beautiful young
Hebe. He advanced a step, stooped, and
picked up the morocco slipper, regarding it
critically. It was small enough to have belonged to Cinderella, or Atalanta—if Atalanta had donned a slipper. At the same
time it was a good deal worn, and looked
peeled and discoloured, as if it had run over
rough stones and damp grass, as well as
soft carpets. Finally, it had been thrust
down at the heel in a flagrantly slip-shod
fashion, for which the wearer had been
punished by her loss. But, poor little

thing, how frightened she had looked!
Was she kept in great order by strict dragons
of mother and elder sisters? That must
have been an elder sister whom he had met
several times, with an air about her as if
she could enforce good manners. Would
the little one be exposed and brought to
book if she were found out? Should he
not screen her to the best of his ability?
He put the disreputable small slipper into
his pocket, and laughed softly. It was the
first personal adventure which had happened
to him since he came to Glasgow. It was
the first thing of the kind that had ever befallen him.

Presently the current of Sir Hugo's medi-
tations was arrested, and he was recalled to
ordinary life by the entrance of the other
men, and the appearance of Mrs. Drysdale,
who had dressed early, because she knew
the picture-gallery would be shown, and she
would be wanted while Tam slipped away
to dress. *She* did not look much like a

dragon, anyhow, Sir Hugo reflected in par-
enthesis, as he was introduced to her, while
he knew from whom the little one had her
lovely face. These Glasgow fellows had the
best of everything.

Mrs. Drysdale, on her side, leapt to the
conclusion that, to be a fine young English
baronet, 'Sir Hughie' seemed an innocent
lad enough—not more alarming than Guy
Horsburgh, who had been a schoolfellow of
young Tam's.

Auld Tam was already turning to the
pictures, 'looking sharp,' and eager to get
through with the job in hand—to introduce
the visitor to the Drysdale Hall collection,
and witness his surprise and pleasure, before
the owner had to go.

'I cannot promise you much, Sir Hugie.
What can one man do? and it seems only
the other day I took to the trade. Young
Tam, there, may gather something worth a
man's coming to see. I have hardly an
auld maister, unless you can call this Keep

—which is doubtful—and that Veroneese fit representatives of the auld schules. To tell the truth, I have not a great eye for their merits. Give me the modern artists that can draw, whose colours are not all gone off to fiddle-broon.'

'But there is your Grooze, Tam, and your Missoneer,' Mrs. Drysdale reminded her husband. 'You're surely forgetting them.'

'No, mother, but they are not auld maisters, more by token Missoneer is living, like Breeton—I've a great wark with Breeton—and Weelems, Sir Hugie. I went out of my way and paid eight hunder doun for a canvas of Breeton's of no great size, as you'll see in a moment; but, man, his peasants are to the life. And there's a Madame Broon here, that I like in her work as well as any woman going. But I must be aff, not to keep the dinner waiting. Mind, mother, the Milly, and do not forget the Wilkie, and the Raeburn, for the honour of auld Scotland. But take care you leave the gentlemen in time to change their feet [boots].'

Mrs. Drysdale did her best with such simplicity and goodwill, that she defied criticism, either on her pronunciation or her art knowledge. Sir Hugo listened with even more than the courtesy natural to him. Presently he turned aside to a flower-stand.

'You have rival colours here, Mrs. Drysdale. What a show of hyacinths you must have! You beat my mother; and she is rather famous for her hyacinths.'

'It is very kind of you to say so, sir,' Mrs. Drysdale acknowledged gratefully. 'But I know Scotland cannot compete with England in garden flooers. We've to send to English nurseries for our best roses and geraniums. But if you like our hyacinths, I wish you had been a little later and seen our rerenunculeses. Tam—that's Maister Drysdale—is very prood of our rerenunculeses. They can do nothing to them at Barley Riggs.'

'Horsburgh, you wretched stickler for a syllable,' Sir Hugo attacked his friend when they were in the privacy of their rooms, 'why did you nearly break down at the " re-renunculeses " ?'

'I cannot tell,' said Horsburgh, grinning again at the recollection. 'She might as well have said "rhinoceroses," when she was at it.'

'You might have upset me,' his companion continued to reproach the offender with youthful severity; 'and rather than have hurt the good soul I would have swallowed all the ranunculuses in the world. Never mind, I saw a vision before you came, in which I am glad you did not share—you were not worthy of it.'

'Claribel or Eppie, I take it. Well, they are both handsome enough girls, in different styles, and they'll have lots of tin.'

'Handsome enough!' echoed Sir Hugo

indignantly, while he did not deign to notice
the mercenary reference to ' tin.'

But he said no more.

In the meantime young Eppie was hiding
her discomfited blushes in her own room,
where she not only blushed, but cried a little,
she felt so ashamed of herself and of the
discredit she had brought on her family.
Then her sense, of which she was by no
means destitute, came to her aid. It was
no such catastrophe after all. Very likely
Sir Hugo had hardly looked at her. She
could not tell what he was like, or what he
wore, further than that he was slim and
brown like Dr. Peter, yet with an air—she
supposed that of a court—which did not
belong to Dr. Peter. Sir Hugo, if it was
Sir Hugo, must have taken off his overcoat,
for he had on a black coat and a white—
was it a white or a black tie ? she had forgotten ; and no doubt he had forgotten all
about her by this time, particularly as he
must have seen she was not grown up.

Then she appeased her tender conscience by assuring herself that she would tell mother all about it, the moment she came into the drawing-room. She—Eppie—would not mind being scolded. Mother's scolding was not hard to bear — it was when she was vexed her young daughter could not stand it.

At this stage of her reflections Eppie was able to turn with renewed interest to her white 'frock'—she called it frock, as her mother did—and the pink ribands she was to wear with it, for the evening.

Clary came in dressed, to see what Eppie was going to make of herself, and did not notice anything amiss with her sister. But Clary, from the æsthetic height of one of her creamy tints, set off by filmy lace, looked disparagingly at Eppie's pure, clear pink ribands.

'Child, I wish you would not always wear pink,' objected Claribel. 'Nicol will bring you some other trimming and put it on for you. I should say some dim blue, or even maize or salmon colour, or pale coral would be better.'

'Thank you, Clary, but I prefer pink,' said Eppie, with a mind of her own.

'You don't know that the colour has gone out,' Clary explained calmly, from the stronghold of her superior information.

'Have roses gone out?' inquired Eppie quickly. Then she coloured, and excused herself—'Oh! Clary, I hope you do not think I'm prideful, and mean that I am like a rose.'

'Prideful! I wish you would not use such words,' exclaimed Clary, more in resigned despair than in active anger. 'But whether you are like a rose or not, you are too pink yourself to wear pink, especially when nobody else is seen in the colour.'

'Mother is seen,' said Eppie, with girlish dignity, 'and I wish to be like her. There is nobody else in the whole world that I should care so much to be like. But neither of us will ever look so well as mother.'

Clary shrugged her white shoulders, then she said good-naturedly :

'I dare say you are right, if my mother would do herself justice. But because she has an old-fashioned fancy, I do not see that is any reason why you should adopt it.'

Eppie shook her head and closed her lips.

Claribel said, with a laugh :

'I suppose you must please yourself, you spoilt child,' and went away.

'As if mother did not set [become] pink, which she wears to please father,' protested Eppie junior; 'and if she sets it, I must set it too, for I am a little like mother. Anyway, I'll wear it to bear her company.'

During dinner, Tam was bent not only on getting everybody to do honour to the good fare, but to do the greater honour because of the expense and trouble with which it had been brought there.

'I believe the takes of salmon are not promising well this year, Sir Hugie; every fish costs five pounds to this day. Let mother help you to another slice, Leddy Semple. The lamb ought to be first-rate, Sir Jeames, from what it fetches. No, we can do nothing to early peas and petawties like these in the garden here, till the end of the month of June, at the sunest; but go into the market and open your purse-strings, and you may have sparrygrass and strawberries in Januar'.'

In vain young Tam, with a heightened colour, exerted himself to get up dinnertable talk in a manner foreign to him, while Clary, in her unruffled beauty, showed the greatest imperturbability. She was impartially agreeable to Dick Semple and Eneas Mackinnon—between whom she sat. At the same time she took approving note of every look and word of Hugo's, where he occupied the place of honour at her mother's right hand. Her observation of the latter was undisturbed by the uncertainty of what Mrs. Drysdale might be saying to the Englishman. Clary's good opinion of herself and her claims helped her to be reasonable. It enabled her to extend an amnesty to her relations for whatever offences they might be guilty of, and to expect the rest of the world to be equally indulgent. Not even the excitement of the aspiration she was indulging, and the rivalry she proposed to enter upon—all in the most maidenly way—could provoke her to lose her balance, or force her to feel nervous, agitated, quickly vexed.

It was worse with auld Tam when the wine, on which he piqued himself, came more to the front. This wine had been round the world, and that had lain in other cellars than his, for more than a century. And here was something from a bin which only he and another man in Glasgy could import, at any sacrifice.

Sir Hugo had to explain, in self-defence

—to save the semicircle of glasses at his
right hand from being filled with a frequency
which only Glasgow heads could stand un-
impaired—that his mother had been captivated with the information that the Prince
Consort, when he first came to England at
the age of seventeen, had drunk nothing
stronger than water. She had taken to
drinking water constantly, that her boy
might be reared as simply. The consequence was that though he had lived to know
what a college ' wine ' meant, it was an
acquired taste with him. He could not in
sincerity profess, though Mr. Drysdale might
well be shocked at his ignorance, that he,
Sir Hugo, knew much more than the first
rudiments of the subject. He was afraid
his mother had rashly imperilled the chance
of his ever becoming a good judge of wines.

Auld Tam stared a little, and it crossed
his mind how many young Glasgow men
would hold their claim to be gentlemen irre-
parably injured by such an admission as Sir

Hugo had not hesitated to make, though he had incurred his disqualification by following the example of a prince.

Then Tam allowed his better nature to come to the front, and be heard on the question.

'Your mither must be a good woman,' he said magnanimously. 'But if she exercised the same strictness with regard to your victuals, I should expect to find you confined to vegetables, like the new sect of vegetarians, or content with bread and cheese instead of roast beef.'

'Oh no! we were not anchorites,' said Sir Hugo, laughing, 'though my mother does not care much what she eats, and she would have been annoyed to see me set great store on my plate when I was a boy. I believe she was tempted to regard schoolboys as a combination of ogres and gourmands; but she always took care that her friends should not suffer from her theories.'

'This is very interesting,' said Lady

Semple. 'I like men and women to strike out original views.'

'But unfortunately this is not original,' said Sir Hugo carelessly. 'It merely means that my mother was a great admirer of the character of the late Prince Consort. She set about trying if she could find anything in his training to account for the satisfactory result. She had the presumption—which may be forgiven in a mother, I suppose—to seek to graft that something on her son's experience.'

'You must have been a great thocht to your mither,' said Mrs. Drysdale simply.

'I am afraid I was,' said Sir Hugo, between jest and earnest; 'an only son generally is.'

'You may say that; I ken it to my cost!' exclaimed Mrs. Drysdale, with a look at young Tam that awoke a laugh.

'My impression is that the conversation is getting too personal—what do you say,

Mr. Tam Drysdale?' Sir Hugo appealed to his fellow-sufferer.

'My mother will tell you that only sons are either deils or daws,' said young Tam.

'I have heard of the deil, and I am acquainted with the daw of Rheims,' said Sir Hugo; 'but what is he doing here? He is not so far removed from a deil as to form a contrast—he is the incarnation of mischief.'

'Oh! but he is a duffer in this instance,' explained young Tam.

'Well, folks may seek to fricht me as they like about Sir Hughie Willoughby being sic a grand young gentleman,' Mrs. Drysdale confided to Lady Semple when the ladies repaired to the drawing-room. 'I'll never heed another word they say. I'm sure he's quite hamely, speaking of his leddy mither, not as "my leddy," but "my mither," as freely as my son Tam might speak of me. I can never think ill of a young lad that is ready to speak of his mither, Lady Semple.'

'Think ill, my dear Mrs. Drysdale! why should you? You must think nothing save good of Sir Hugo. I am sure he is most anxious to win your favour.'

'It is very good of you to say so, my leddy,' said Eppie senior, with smiling incredulity. 'But what for should he care to have my favour? A fine gentleman has more in his head. He was very pleasant all the denner-time, I will say that for him; but I was not so besotted as not to see he would have been the better of anither pairtner than an auld wife. I kenned it was ane of the rules of gude company that he should take me into the dining-room, but I grudged the needcessity for him—'deed did I. He would have been far better waured on one of the young leddies that are ready to look sweet on him —and I dinna blame them, for he's a maist comely, civil-spoken lad.'

'My dear Mrs. Drysdale,' Lady Semple protested again, 'you must not depreciate yourself in this. fashion. What are you thinking of? You must not call yourself. "an auld wife." Why, you'll be teaching Dick the trick, to practise on me before I know what I'm about. I am sure you are ever so many years younger than I am, and I can tell you I do not mean to be set aside, in the light of an old woman, for a dozen years to come.'

'But the young folk maun have their day, and take our place,' pleaded Eppie's soft voice. 'What have we to do, Leddy Semple, but make room for them, and prood to do it?'

'Here is somebody that will not be made room for,' said Lady Semple, coming down on young Eppie, before she could spring from the hearth-rug, on which she had been sitting basking in the glow of the fire—not unwelcome in the chillness of the April evening—'somebody in no hurry

to grow up and render her elders super-
annuated.   Eppie, do you call your mother
an old woman ?'

'Mother old!' cried Eppie, in mingled
indignation and alarm, 'she will not be
old till I am old myself; at least, not till I
am thirty or forty.   Father is eight years
older than mother, and he is only a middle-
aged man.'

'Listen to her!   That is right, child.
I hope Dick will swear as fervently by my
youthfulness.'

The moment Sir Hugo entered the drawing-room, his eyes fell on young Eppie,
and he tried to get near her.   She appeared to him a more Hebe-like vision than
before—twice as lovely as he had imagined
her.   In vain Clary waited for him, keeping others at a distance.   In vain Guy
Horsburgh, tired of the suavities of both
the Miss Vaughans, sought mischievously
to draw his friend into their neighbourhood, so that Guy might escape honourably

from his station to more attractive quarters, by bringing within reach of the arrows showered fruitlessly upon him a more illustrious, perhaps more vulnerable, prey. In vain Athole Murray, who was there without Dr. Peter, called away to a patient, was stirred by young Tam's discontent to glance with lively curiosity at Prince Charming. *He* only wanted to be introduced to young Eppie.

In the meantime the girl, with the weight of trouble on her mind for what had happened before dinner, flitted about the room, to escape the guest of the evening, in the style of a restless fairy. She was here and there and everywhere, like an uncanny will-o'-the-wisp, telling herself, all the time, that it was a very hard and perverse chance which made the grand gentleman torment her by coming in her way.

At last her father arrested Eppie by putting his hand on her shoulder, with the surprised exclamation :

'Bairn! have you turned yourself into
a bird, happing from branch to branch?'
The next moment he wheeled her round
face to face with the enemy. 'It is my
little girl Eppie, Sir Hugie. Eppie, this
is Sir Hugie Willoughby,' said auld Tam,
in his singleness of heart.

There was no help for it. She could
not run away again; she had to behave as
if she had been Clary. She heard the
young man mutter something of having
had the pleasure of seeing Miss Eppie
Drysdale before. But it was a slip of the
tongue. He did not say another word
which could betray the smallest inclination
to expose her. He did not even speak of
pictures or flowers. He only asked her if
she liked yachting, and had ever spent
two or three days at sea—idle questions,
evidently for the purpose of making conversation. They could have no reference
to the grievous scandal of his having found
her, when it was time for the guests to

assemble in the picture-gallery, with dirty hands, 'towsy' hair, and a torn frock, and of her having run off, without waiting to beg his pardon, leaving such an old slipper behind her.

As Eppie saw oblivion settling down on the scrape she had got into, she began to recover her courage, to look Sir Hugo in the face, and to think, like her mother, that he was not so grand, and not 'fearsome' at all. He seemed younger than young Tam, and kind and merry. She was ready to commit more solecisms by chattering to him of 'Beardie,' her Newfoundland, 'White Breeks,' Barley Riggs and all the beasts there, little deaf Willie Finlay, the Glasgow shops, and whatever else came into her head, when she was prevented by somebody calling upon her to sing.

For young Eppie's gift of singing native ballads was already so decided, and so well known, that where it was concerned, she had broken the chrysalis of her nonage.

She was accustomed to make such music
wherever it was in request—at home, at
Barley Riggs, even at Semple Barns, without thought or fear, as a matter of course.
Clary would play the accompaniments, and
Eppie would sing, in her fresh, sweet,
tuneful voice, 'Logan Braes,' or 'The
bonnie, bonnie broom o' Cowdenknowes,'
a room full of people hanging on her
notes, as on the carol of some wonderful
bird.

To-night she sang a quaint, old-fashioned
ditty—which was a favourite of auld Tam's,
and for that matter of young Eppie's. It
had some appropriateness to those who
knew the singer. It began with the wistful appeal of a mother to her son—probably
an only son, like Sir Hugo or young Tam :

> ' Whaur ha'e you been a' day,
>   My boy Tammy ?
> Whaur ha'e you been a' day,
>   My boy Tammy ?'

Tammy, thus adjured, has the candour
and tender tact to reply :

'I've been by burn and flowery brae,
Meadow green and mountain grey,
Courtin' o' this young thing,
    Just come frae her mammy.'

The mother, not unpropitiated, goes on to ask :

'An' whaur got ye that young thing,
    My boy Tammy?
Whaur got ye that young thing,
    My boy Tammy?'

To which the son gives answer:

'I got her doon in yonder howe,
Smiling on a bonny knowe,
Herding ae wee lamb an' ewe
    For her puir mammy.'

Then he makes a frank statement of his wooing of 'the young thing,' with her resistance to his suit and naïve assertion of the claims of his powerful rival:

'The smile gaed aff her bonnie face,
    "I mauna leave my mammy ;
She's gi'en me meat, she's gi'en me claes,
She's been my comfort a' my days ;
My father's death brocht monie waes—
    I canna leave my mammy." '

The difficulty is triumphantly overcome by
the lover's generosity :

> ' " We'll tak' her hame and mak' her fain,
>   My ain kind-hearted lammie ;
> We'll gi'e her meat, we'll gi'e her claes,
> We'll be her comfort a' her days."
> The wee thing gi'es her hand, an' says,
>   "There, gang an' ask my mammy." '

The little drama winds up with the approving question from the other mother—
large-hearted like her son :

> ' Has she been to the kirk wi' thee,
>   My boy Tammy ?
> Has she been to the kirk wi' thee,
>   My boy Tammy ?'

To which there is the glad, soft assurance :

> ' She has been to the kirk wi' me,
>   An' the tear was in her e'e ;
> For oh ! she's but a young thing,
>   Just come frae her mammy.'

Mrs. Drysdale furtively wiped her eyes,
auld Tam cleared his throat ; Sir Hugo
listened like one entranced, and haunted
Eppie till the party broke up.

'I did not know Willoughby was so fond of music,' Guy Horsburgh turned the matter over in his mind.

'Talk of Sir Hugo not giving himself airs!' said one of the Vaughan sisters. 'What do you call a young man's neglecting grown-up people to amuse himself with an unformed child, if such conduct cannot be classed as airs?'

'He's making his way with the little one as one means of getting at Claribel. I don't know that it is necessary, and I did not think that young men had been so modest nowadays, but it is refreshing that it is so,' Lady Semple settled dogmatically.

Claribel witnessed the first secession from the ranks of her admirers, the first preference on the part of one of them for her younger sister, with a shade of wonder, but with no other visible emotion, unless it were a tinge of amusement. She was so completely mistress of herself that she gave no sign of responding to the dog-like devo-

tion of Eneas Mackinnon stepping forward
to fill once more the vacant place—from
which he had been at no distant date un-
ceremoniously ousted—looking at her with
long, wistful looks. She only made an
easy suggestion :

‘Will you help me with this portfolio,
Mr. Mackinnon ? There are some water-
colour sketches in it, which my father
bought the other day, that I should like to
show to Lady Semple. Thanks. Do you
care to see them too ? Oh, if you like.’

That night Clary, in her dressing-gown,
went into her sister's room, where Eppie
was combing her hair, with her eyes
closing.

‘What is it, Clary ?’ asked Eppie in
surprise, starting round wide awake. ‘Is
there anything the matter ?’

‘Nothing at all,’ answered Clary lightly,
and began talking and laughing over the
events of the evening—how people had
looked and spoken, how much improved

Guy Horsburgh was. Then she asked what was Eppie's opinion of Sir Hugo, now that she had seen him.

Eppie was quite ready to give it. He was just like other people, she thought, only a good deal nicer. Could it be possible that he had such a wonderful old house, and was cousin to an earl, and might go to Court and speak to the Queen?

'Be spoken to by her, you mean,' corrected Clary.

'Well, isn't it the same thing?' asked unsophisticated Eppie. 'I did not have time to ask him about the Queen. I don't think he would have minded though I had. He looked as if he would be easier to live with than our Tam—not that I would like to change Tam, though he is dorty sometimes,' with sudden relenting towards her brother.

'I don't suppose Sir Hugo understands what "dorty" means,' said Clary, raising her eyebrows.

'Oh! but you're wrong, Clary,' said Eppie very decidedly; 'he told me that he understood every word I sang. He had read Burns, and was fond of Sir Walter. I was just going to ask him which was his favourite character in the Waverley Novels, when Mr. Horsburgh came to say the trap was at the door.'

'You may have another opportunity of asking him,' said Clary, a little vaguely. 'In the meantime, I came in to tell you that you sang your best, and looked very well in your white and pink. I am not sure that pink is not the most becoming colour for you, after all. But I should like you to have a pink *crêpe de chine*, or something of that sort, made by Madame Sophie. Pink and silver,' repeated Clary, with the air of a connoisseur; 'I think that would suit you.'

'Oh, Clary!' was all that Eppie could say, for she was by no means insensible to the promotion.

Clary's dressmaker and pink *crêpe de chine*
and silver—the very idea was a high compliment.

'You see I am proud of my pretty little
sister, though I don't wish to make her
vain,' said Clary, kissing Eppie with real
affection, before the elder lighted her candle
and disappeared.

Eppie gasped.   Clary proud of her!
She lay awake for fully ten minutes
puzzling over the flattering problem.   She
had always known that Clary liked her, in
the light of their near relationship, though
Clary tormented her with plans for im-
provement, and made her furious by proposing to send her away from home.   Still
Clary was sorry when she—Eppie—was
ill, and did her best for her, and proved to
her that her sister was fond of her in Clary's
quiet, self-occupied fashion.   But ' proud '
was a very different feeling—proud of
little, Scotch-speaking, blundering Eppie,
with her lack of accomplishments !

Eppie felt bound in honour to tell Clary what had happened in the picture-gallery. The girl took the next opportunity when she and Clary happened to be in the garden together the following morning. But Clary only laughed, and said:

'Never mind—what could have put it into your head to run away? Don't do it again. On the contrary, you ought to learn to make the best of yourself. But though it would not look well in me to be childish and silly, I don't believe either Sir Hugo or any other man will take it ill on your part.'

Clary was not speaking sarcastically— she was in perfect good faith.

Eppie did not gasp again, but she lingered behind by the violet-bed, letting Clary stroll on. In truth, Eppie was over-come by the delicious consciousness of some attraction in her which disarmed hostility. She knew she was like her mother, for everybody said so. Therefore

she must be a little bonnie, but she had
never suspected that she was so bonnie as
Clary's words seemed to imply. The discovery did not fill Eppie's head with nonsense, as her father and mother would have
said; for she began, after a moment's
innocent elation, to distrust the existence
of youthful beauty, and to seek to under-
value it, if it were there. She was well
enough; she might be rather bonnie, inas-
much as she had a share of mother's looks;
but for the rest, it was only a foolish fancy
of Clary's, for which Eppie was much
obliged to her sister, and would always
like her the better for it. *She* was handsome, like a picture, like a queen. Eppie
would never look like that—not that it
mattered very much when beauty was only
skin-deep, and people liked each other just
as well without it. Would father and
mother care for her a grain less though she
were to be seized with small-pox to-morrow,
and be left a disfigured object for the rest

of her days? There was Athole Murray.
Everybody said, and Eppie's eyes told her,
that Athole was plain, in spite of her eyes,
with a wide mouth and a dumpy nose;
but then she was so clever and nice; and
Eppie shrewdly suspected, if nobody else
did, that young Tam would sooner have a
pleasant word from Athole Murray's witty
tongue than all the smiles of all the beauties
in Glasgow.

The truth was, Clary had seen Eppie
with another person's eyes, and her own
were too reasonable to remain sealed in
such a case. She had received an enlightenment. It was the first tribute, little
as Eppie suspected it, to the possibility of
her becoming Lady Willoughby of Willoughby Court, or some equally distinguished person, and Clary was ready
to pay the tribute. There was nothing
grudging or unmagnanimous in the young
woman's pride.

'Tam,' Mrs. Eppie confided to her

husband in the privacy of their luxurious chamber, after she had sung the praises of Sir Hugo till she had nearly sung auld Tam asleep, ' did you not see that he was ta'en with our bairn ?'

' What, Clary !' cried Tam, rousing himself to the dawning glory of becoming father-in-law to a baronet and squire of many acres.

' No, Eppie ; the lamb, who had no more thocht of what was in the lad's mind than when she was a wee thing playing round my knee.'

' Then leave her without the thocht,' said Tam gruffly. ' For shame, woman, to even a lassock like her to a lad of ony kind, aboon a' to a lad by richts no in her ain station—here the day, and awa' the morn ! She's not dreaming of lads, and you may catch her leal licht heart and brush the bloom aff, like the dew from the gowans in the morning, and break it before she's weel in her teens.'

'I never said I would breathe a word o't to her, Tam; I would not be so bold. A young lassie's heart is like the kirk itsel' —no to be lichtly entered,' said Mrs. Drysdale reproachfully; 'and what for should I seek to promote sic a distinction for little Eppie? Lifted up and lonely, and torn from a' her frien's; her that is friendly and fond of her ain folk! You and me never to see her again, or ken richt how she's farin', unless aince or twice in as mony years! All the same, the fine lad's ta'en with the bairn. You may tak' my word for it, Tam.'

'And all the same, you would gie her to him, and hae your reward in kennin' young Eppie a fine leddy, though everything were to happen as you say.'

'I would not stand in her road, Tam; nor would you,' said Mother Eppie, with spirit.

'Have it any way you like then, and let me sleep,' said auld Tam, with a pretence at despair. 'But mind, the felly's going back to Cambridge in little more than a week, and there's small chance of our seeing his face again, even if he had not uncles and aunties, and what not, to come forrit and cry out at his demeaning himsel' to think of matching his title with a bleacher and dyer's dochter.'

'He's coming back to see mair of Scotland and Glasgy in the Long Vacation. I heard him say that mysel'; and he's of age and his ain maister, with a gude mither, that Leddy Semple says would never conter him in onything he set his heart on, that was richt! And you ken, Tam, you're a man in a big way—no just a common bleacher and dyer; while you've often telled me bleachin' and dyein' and calico-printin' will come to the front of the treds. You can gie your twa lasses muckle tochers. No doubt I would be wae for my bonnie bairn to gang so far awa' from me, where I could not see her sweet face ilka day of my life,

though she would never forget you and
me, however we were sindered, for a' her
grandeur—that I'll come bund for. But,
eh, Tam, to think of our ain little Eppie
being "my leddy"!'

'Hoot, awa' with you, big Eppie! you're
takin' leave of your senses!' Tam put an
end to the conversation.

But though he was too much of a man
to own it, the feminine ambition tickled
him mightily. He fell asleep and dreamt
—now of saying an eternal farewell to his
darling—now of seeing her with a coronet
on her head (it was easy to change a
baronet into a baron in a dream)—on her
way to a State ball at Buckingham Palace,
or the opening of the House of Lords, he
was not sure which.

CHAPTER XXI.

BEFORE Sir Hugo quitted Glasgow and returned to Cambridge, he rode out and paid
a call at Drysdale Hall, instead of leaving
his card. But he was not shown into the
picture-gallery. No Cinderella was about
the drawing-room or the hall. Indeed, he
was unfortunate in missing both of the
daughters of the house, who were in Glasgow. He only saw Mrs. Drysdale, and his
solitary small consolation was in earnestly
recommending himself to that friendly
woman.

During this conversation, Sir Hugo
caught at the casual mention of a lecture
on Health, to be given by Dr. Peter Murray
to the workpeople at Drysdale Haugh, at

which some of the members of their em-
ployer's family were to be present. He was
not familiar with any lectures except university lectures. He had never been at a
lecture to operatives. He had heard of
Dr. Peter Murray as an original—not a
mute, but a comparatively inglorious—man
of learning and science.

The young Englishman worried Guy
Horsburgh into taking him to listen to
what Guy was persuaded was not in
Sir Hugo's line; anyhow, Sir Hugo was
punished for his pains. The lecture was
clever and well delivered, as well as homely
and practical. Moreover, the operatives
came to hear it. Among them was Lady
Semple, whose last hobby was hygiene.
But the deputation from Drysdale Hall
consisted of auld Tam and young Tam,
who had got up the lecture, and Mrs. Drysdale, who accompanied her husband from
pure love of his company, and because she
owed Athole Murray a visit.

After all, the scene of Dr. Peter's lecture was not a likely place in which to meet Clary and Eppie. But in spite of the unreasonableness of his expectations, Sir Hugo felt a good deal disgusted by their nonfulfilment, and for a time put up his back at the whole affair, in a manner that would have tended to impair his universal popularity, had not his genial temper recovered itself before it was too late. Then, in the revulsion of feeling, he began to admire the lecture, the lecturer, the audience of respectable, hard-headed, sound-hearted working men and women almost as extravagantly as he had admired everything in Glasgow. And the young man was positively enchanted with Barley Riggs, to which he and his friend Horsburgh went, on the hospitable invitation of Dr. Peter, to have a cup of tea with Lady Semple and the Drysdales at Miss Murray's tea-table, before they returned home to dinner.

Sir Hugo had no particular thirst for tea,

but the enthusiastic side of his temperament was caught by the new surroundings. He had only twice before made the acquaintance of establishments equally plain and simple, and at the same time bearing unmistakable marks of culture—once when he was at school in Germany, and once in the house of a professor at Harvard, which he had visited during a tour in America the previous summer. In each case he had fallen violently in love with the example. What appeared to Sir Hugo the quaint homeliness, together with the real refinement, and in the case of Barley Riggs, the little foreign touches which showed that a man had travelled afar and yet kept faithful to his first love, seized hold of his impulsive fancy, just as Eppie Drysdale's rusticity and exquisite sweetness had captivated the same rampant imagination.

Sir Hugo persuaded himself that *le grand simple* was his *beau idéal*, that he cared little for the local standing and antiquarian glory of Willoughby Court—at least, that if he were not Sir Hugo, he would be a young Dr. Peter, and that, on the whole, he would prefer to be a Dr. Peter. He was sure that he would like, above all things, to have such a study, parlour, and living-room as that at Barley Riggs, to be waited on by a single rosy-cheeked maid-servant, to go and come when he chose, to be refreshed by tea and a poached egg, or a slice of mutton ham, instead of a dinner of half a dozen courses. The notion belonged to the attributes which had rendered Sir Hugo, ten years before, the most eager young mock Robinson Crusoe that ever sprang from a high civilization. He was very boyish still, in spite of his easy good-breeding and his having come into his kingdom. What young Eppie Drysdale called 'the heap of beasts' at Barley Riggs was as fascinating to him as to her. It was night, and they were most of them in their sheds and roosts; but a few streamed forth

—sidling, fluttering, barking, mewing, twit-
tering—to hail their owners. Sir Hugo
would have liked to provide himself with
Dr. Peter's lantern and go round on a tour
of inspection. The lovely moonlight in
some respects supplied the place of the lantern, and shone white on the wealth of spring
flowers and on the cribs and perches of the
animals.

There must be something subtle and in-
toxicating in moonlight; if not in all moonlight, in special kinds, such as that which
shone on Barley Riggs this night, and got
into the brains of all the younger persons
present, so that Dr. Peter could hardly keep
them in order. They would not rest at
Athole's tea-table, nor could its mistress be
said to do much to detain them. She fulfilled her duties, certainly, but when they
were done she was on the wing like the
others, not to lose the moonlight; as if
moonlight were not cheap and common—
almost as much so as sunshine—to be had

on so many fine nights a month, the whole
year round, during all the years of all the
centuries. No doubt there were favourable
conditions which were not always available,
such as weather unusually balmy for a Scotch
spring, a pleasant garden to wander in, a
group of young people—three young men
and two girls, for Athole had a Glasgow girl
visiting her—thrown together by chance,
and suddenly developing undreamed-of
elements of good fellowship. When these
extraordinary advantages did occur, perhaps
it was well to improve the occasion. It
might have been the fact of having been
caged up with the rest of the assembly for
an hour in a schoolroom, listening to a
lecture of any kind, and then let loose like
so many school-children. It might have
been latent impulses stirring young hearts.
Whatever the reason, these older boys and
girls, all of them, including young Tam,
were gay and unrestrained. They made
much merry movement and noise as they

tramped and flitted about the garden; stooped to examine and insist upon the points of flowers and vegetables; were mad enough to seek for birds' nests by the moonbeams, and disturbed the domestic privacy of two broods of ducks and chickens and a litter of puppies, to expatiate and dispute on the rival merits of the flabby, woolly specimens.

At length, the quieter company within doors—Dr. Peter, Lady Semple, auld Tam, and Mrs. Drysdale—were brought to the door to see what the commotion was about, whether treasure-trove had turned up in the garden, or treason was being plotted in the usually peaceful domain.

Athole Murray, Sir Hugo, and young Tam were the ringleaders. Athole's friend and Guy Horsburgh were merely serving as echoes. Athole was marching between her two squires, and was bantering them impartially. Did Sir Hugo really approve of the moon? Had he ever gone a-hunting by its light? Had he shot a wandering calf for a stag royal? Was Mr. Tom prepared to treat moonlight as a colour, and to bring it out in chemicals? There were moonlight beads, why not moonlight calicoes? Might she be allowed to draw the pattern, and call it the lunatic design?

Both the young men were answering her in the same vein, and young Tam was speaking as briskly and with as much idle glee as Sir Hugo spoke; the moonlight had touched and transformed him. For the moment he was as unthinking and unheeding as a young man need be. The inequalities of life had ceased to exist for him. He was impervious to his own lack of desert and hopelessness of attaining his ends. He feared nothing, and anticipated nothing.

Snatches of the senseless gaiety, which was getting slightly wild, reached the listeners, and coming from certain sources bewildered the hearers. Mrs. Drysdale, especially, was much exercised by what she saw and heard, and confided her perplexity to its natural recipient on the drive homeward.

' I have always had a regard for that lassie of Dr. Peter's,' she began slowly; ' for one thing, she's a mitherless lassie, and she has played her part well, and been a gude housekeeper and a gude dochter to her father— honest man. I have aye thought her a fine lassie, beyond the common, with her management, and industry, and sense, though maybe Dr. Peter has spoiled her with learnin'; yet she's not conceited. I never reckoned her anythin' but modest and unaffected, and as gude company as if she had never opened a book. But, weel-a-wat she's no bonnie— a blecket thing with a muckle mouth. What a fine lad and grand gentleman like Sir Hughie can see in her, to daff [jest] with her as he war doin' the night, passes my comprehension.'

' Every man to his mind,' said Tam a

little stiffly. 'But your new friend Sir Hugie seems to have a variety of minds. However. he's welcome. Nobody will object.'

'Oh, I pay little heed to a lad, whatever his rank, bein' led awa' by a bit of funnin' with a lass, and enjoyin' it at his age,' said Mrs. Drysdale quickly. 'More by token, there was nobody he liked better standin' by; and I'm willin' to make every allowance for a lassie such as Athole Murray—a clever lassie with a quick tongue that lives alane with an auld man, hooever fond she may be of him, and is fain to get her head out with her kind, whiles. But what troubles me is that she has the face to laugh at oor Tam, who is so far aboon her in his solidity and superiority, as if he had been ony triflin' lad like Sir Hughie.'

'If you noticed so much as that, mother,' said Tam with decision, 'you might have gone farther and seen that the felly did not find faut with bein' laughed at by her; he was carryin' her on as if the joke were marry to his banes.'

'It would hae been a pity in him to condescend to be wrathful,' said Eppie, holding her head high ; ' but she should mind what she's about, and no' take sic liberties—they are no' becomin' in a young lass.'

' And so should he mind,' corrected Tam, holding the scales more evenly between the offending parties, and speaking sharply, ' for this will never do.'

' What will never do, Tam ?' cried Eppie, in a high key of mingled indignation and derision. ' Have you gane gyte [lost your senses] ? Do you think for a moment that oor Tam, who has but to wag his finger to have the bonniest, brawest lassie, with the biggest tocher in Glasgy, could be in earnest in makin' up to a plain-lookin', ill-dressed lassie like Athole Murray ?'

' You women think owre muckle of looks and claes [dress],' protested Tam.

' Well, it's the first time I've heard you

men cast laith at them,' declared Eppie
sarcastically.

'Onyway,' cried Tam, 'there's mair roads
to a man's heart than by his een—and mair
roads to please them in, too, than by lily
skins and red cheeks, strecht noses and wee
mous—though these are all gude things of
their kind. I'm no' disputin' it. I'm the
last man that should dispute it—eh, Eppie,
my doo! But I dare say, if it were examined into, men like Tam are as often
caught by their lugs [ears] as by their
een, and you'll own that lassie has a tongue
that would wile a bird from a tree.'

'I own naething of the sort,' said
Mother Eppie, fairly nettled; 'a tongue
that would clip cloots [cut cloth], if that is
what you mean. I never heard sic nonsense
as you've been speakin' the nicht, Tam.'

'I expected you to say sae,' said Tam
composedly; 'yet not five minutes syne
you were praising the lass to the masthead
—you began by not findin' words gude

enough to wale upon her. And you were richt,' said Tam, with sudden emphasis. ' She's a perfect leddy—as my auld friend, whom I'm proud to call sae, Dr. Peter, is every inch a gentleman ; she's a lass among a thousand. Dod! when I think of what she did for the auld Miss Mackinnons, I could find it in my heart not only to waur [spend] Tam upon her, but to count him not half gude enough for her, and a happy and honoured man if he could get her.'

' Tam, oor Tam !' gasped poor Mrs. Drysdale, overcome by the infatuation of another of her men-folk. ' But you never thocht enough of my fine sedate lad. The lassie's weel enough, forbye she has not a mither. I never said an ill word of her ; but you're clean daft about her—a black-a-viced [dark complexioned] thing. I would not give a five-pound note for every steek [stitch] in her possession.'

' You need not fash your head, Eppie, my woman,' said Tam more soberly. ' If a man lives in the world, he has to use the world's measurements. I ken what folk would think and say. For all Athole Murray's gudeness and cleverness, and though she's a leddy born and bred, they would hold her as little better than a mill-hand or a bleacher—a plain-headed, insignificant-looking lass, without a penny, that drew patterns for the pattern-shop. They would say that young Tam had demeaned himself, instead of risin' a step higher in the world. Na, na; it will not do. Whether young Tam and her are wooin' Scotch fashion, or waging war, there must be an end of it. She's a gude dochter, and a word to Dr. Peter would be enough, as I would let the chiel, who'll never have done with his maggots [whims], ken on the deafest side of his head. But I want no unpleasantness with an old friend that I can help. The folly may blow over, or die a natural death of itself; or the lassie, who has wit enough to see round a corner, may

put an end to it by havin' no more to say
to the perverse beggar.'

'Athole Murray no more to say to young
Tam!' echoed young Tam's mother almost
faintly, in her horror at the supposition.
She was unable to add any more stinging
suggestion than what was summed up in
Miss Janet Mackinnon's favourite protest,
' Set her up!'

Lady Semple had her version of the
garden scene, which she confided to the
pages of her diary.

'That boy, Sir Hugo, does need somebody to look after him. I wish Claribel
Drysdale would be quick in taking him in
hand, or she may lose her chance, and there
may be other losses. Is he falling in love
all round, as an introduction to a grand
passion for Claribel? These introductions
are not always to be trusted. It was all
very well to pay his devoirs to the little
sister, and ensure her being on his side, but
what has Miss Murray got to do with it?

There is something piquante about that girl —the dangerous fascination which enables some plain women to get the better of all the pretty ones. I am not sure that if she cared she might not be a greater social success than Claribel—more original, racier. But the thing is not to be thought of for a moment. The plain daughter of a country doctor, without the ghost of a fortune! It would be using poor dear Lady Willoughby quite too badly to entertain the idea for a second—indeed, not to take strong steps to guard against it, if it were not that Sir Hugo is going back to his tutor in a week at the latest. (I wish the man joy of his charge; such romantic boys are nearly as bad as *mauvais sujets;* I am glad Dick's romance has taken a different form.) Besides, Dr. Peter Murray is the soul of honour; there is nothing to be feared from him; on the contrary, if he dreamed of such an absurdity, I do believe he would be the first to put a stop to it.'

It was true that Dr. Peter took Athole to task—very gently, however, and in a few words—before the night was over.

'My dear, I think you let your spirits run away with you. In the first place, you ought to have stayed in the house and entertained the married ladies. Then one of them was Lady Semple, and though she sets little store on her rank, in a general way, that is no reason why we should do the same. You ought to have kept Annie [Athole's visitor] with you, and left the lads to divert themselves as they liked in the moonlit garden. There was no great harm done, but it was not like you to be so——'

'So "royd"' [foolishly gay].

Athole took the word out of his mouth, using one of the Doric expressions which the Drysdale Haugh mothers applied to their riotous children. She shook her head and smiled a little, while her face was pale, as if the reflection of the moonlight was still upon it.

'I don't know what came over me.   I
suppose I wanted a " rallyie " [frolic], as
girls like Jeannie say in self-defence.   It was
ill-judged and ill-bred.   I shall take care it
does not happen again ; but one has such a
desire sometimes to cast care—which means
decorum in this instance—to the winds, let
one's spirits loose, and give the reins to the
impulse of the moment—in fact, to be carried
away like a mad creature for five minutes—
when one is pretty sure to be brought up by
some scrape, and feel sorry and ashamed for
the next twenty-four hours.'

As for the two men who had matched
Athole, one of them, young Tam, was not
well out of her presence before he suffered a
collapse.

Sir Hugo held out longer. 'Miss Murray
is simply charming,' he told Guy Horsburgh
with effusion, provoking Guy to cry, 'Hold,
enough ! Willoughby, we'll have you in
ecstasies with my grandmother next.'

CHAPTER XXII.

RORY OF THE SHELTIES COME ALIVE AGAIN.

SIR HUGO WILLOUGHBY had gone back to Cambridge, vowing fervently to return in the course of the summer. The injustice done to him was that everybody did not treat his vows as they deserved, but called to mind the cynical assertion that promises are, like pie-crust, made to be broken.

The Drysdales' set in Glasgow, with Drysdale Hall and Semple Barns, had returned to their normal interests. The individual who, in the end, was the least disturbed by the advent of Sir Hugo, who had most nearly forgotten him, was young Eppie. She was more occupied with the annual transfer of the family for the month of June, from Drysdale Hall to 'Glasgow down the water,' with the daily visits to the pier to see her father go and come, the mornings when she was to wile him away from Glasgow, that he might spend them with her and her mother on the Clyde; the evenings when she was to coax him to take out Beardie to scour the hills or the sands. Her mind was more engrossed with a Newhaven fishwife's costume of pink and white and dark blue, which Clary had actually encouraged her to get, and with the sea-mew's wing which young Tam had given to her. These shining attractions were enough to supersede all the grand young English squires and baronets that had ever existed for young Eppie yet.

Trade was undergoing a shrinking process after its tremendous expansion. The horizon was already clouding over for many of the speculators. Auld Tam was not without a premonition that he also had been over-daring, and too splendidly far-reaching in

his schemes. He might need all his resources before the ends met. Still he had
no fear. He would weather the back-
draught of the tide, when the high waters
of prosperity had ebbed to the lowest mark
of adversity—that as a matter of course ;
he would also ride triumphantly, as he had
always done, over every obstacle.

No, auld Tam's troubles at this time were
still born in the bosom of his family. Young
Tam, though he went on steadily enough
with the business, and began to be an
efficient aid to his father, disappointed him
all the more by continuing to keep out of
society, and to do all his visiting at Barley
Riggs, as if that were the sole house he
cared to visit. Auld Tam could not find
that his son received any encouragement
beyond the merest friendly hospitality. Indeed, Athole was not even ostensibly
friendly. Perhaps it would have been safer
if she had been a calm matter-of-fact friend,
rather than a jesting foe—not always so

much in jest that there was not a spice of
wayward earnestness in her hostility.   As
for Dr. Peter, in the innocence of his heart,
he suspected no ulterior motive ; and auld
Tam hated to be the man to open his friend's
eyes and to reveal himself in a new character,
that of the tyrannical parent and hardened
man of the world.   Claribel, too, was fret-
ting her father.   After the brief interlude
of Sir Hugo's passing across the stage,
when she had turned round and paused,
in a waiting attitude, for what fortune might
bring her, she had gone back—not so much
into receiving Eneas Mackinnon's attentions,
for he did not take it upon him to pay her
attentions which he could not vindicate by
a statement of his prospects next day—but
by the accepting of his mute allegiance.
She was getting herself associated with
him, talked of in connection with him.
Lady Semple was beginning to look grave,
to forbid Dick to bring his friend so constantly to Semple Barns if Claribel was

there, and to give them separate partners at dinner.

The fact that Tam had helped the old Miss Mackinnons in their strait, only served to incense him further with their grand-nephew, for having the consummate audacity, while he passed for the most modest of men, to dangle after Clary, constitute himself her dumb waiter, the peg for her opera-cloak or shawl, the fetcher and carrier of her bouquet and fan, the runner of her errands, the trainer of her dog, the consulting physician of her horse. It was not that auld Tam had not the justice to admit that young Mackinnon's position, in the absence of money, crippled him cruelly from doing anything worth speaking of either for his aunts or for himself. But it was the fact that in such desperate circumstances he had the assurance and selfishness to admire Clary, and get round a sensible, high-spirited girl like her, until he was tempting her to peril her brilliant prospects, which enraged her father.

If she did not take care she would find that she had gone too far to stop without incurring the accusation of being a flirt and a jilt, and there were few reputations a woman could earn that appeared more odious in her father's eyes.

But to interfere in the affairs of a girl so calm, so much the mistress of herself and the situation as Clary was, in order to tell her one or two wholesome truths, was an exercise of a father's duties almost as repugnant to Tam as he found the obligation of hinting to Dr. Peter that Tam's son went too often to Barley Riggs, and ought not to be encouraged in such a waste of time. Fancy Clary's large, rather light eyes, the most defective feature in her face, fixed on her father's with a mesmerizing effect. while he, and not she, was the agitated person! Imagine her voice, in slightly ironical accents, telling him in the spirit, if not in the letter, that she was quite able to take care of herself, he need not trouble his head about her—she knew perfectly well what she was doing!

One May evening, just before dinner, Tam was in the business-room which he had got fitted up for himself at Drysdale Hall. It was a very different place from his office in Glasgow or his office at Drysdale Haugh Works. The common use to which it was put was that of interviewing and paying the wages of domestic servants; but beyond this, it indicated Drysdale Hall to be a landed estate, and the master of Drysdale Hall a laird. Tam, like most traders who have acquired land, had, as has been said, a special pride in his fields and in all that related to them. He relished playing at laird and farmer, and was nearly as bent on heading the markets and agricultural shows with his crops and cattle, as on witching the world by his dyes and printing. His business-room was supplied with samples of seeds and grain, while the walls were hung round with such illustrations of succulent roots, and reaping and sowing machines, and such likenesses of fat cattle as one sees at railway stations in agricultural counties. A spud, with which Tam sometimes armed himself on the rare occasions when he spent an idle morning at home, stood in a corner.

Tam would sit among these suggestive touches, as a Justice of the Peace, in addition to being the master of Drysdale Hall, and dispense law after the fashion of Sir Thomas Lucy. But he was decidedly popular both as a laird and a magistrate—to an extent far more than is usual in a self-made man. A sense of his accessibility which prosperity had not diminished, of his freedom from assumption and pretence which existed side by side with his simple—one is tempted to say honest—vanity, of his inflexible fairness and human-hearted kindliness, more than outweighed the grudge at his rise in life and magnificent success.

As a result of his popularity, Tam was

subjected to intrusions from other persons than policemen, poachers, and county depredators generally. He was apt to be called upon to arbitrate *ex officio* between his humbler neighbours in the country, as between his bigger neighbours in the town. He had no doubt that he was required to judge between such a pair of brethren when two men of the lower class, but sufficiently unlike each other in most things, were shown into his sanctum, unattended by any member of the rural police, on the evening in question. Both men were Highlanders, but it was a few minutes before Tam recognised the able-bodied fellow to be Sir James Semple's dog-man. The other, a miserable scarecrow, with a wild eye, shambled as he walked, and lugged under the arm of his faded tartan coat a battered knapsack.

'Well, lads, what complaint have you to ludge, or advice to seek, the nicht?' asked Tam courteously. 'Stop, are you not one of Sir Jeames's folk? I thocht so. Are

they all well at Semple Barns ?   Now, what
have you to say ?'

'It's no me that has onything to say, Mr.
Drysdale,' said the voluble Sandy Macnab,
immediately becoming spokesman.   'It is
this cratur that Bawby Sed, the trailin',
clashin' [gadding, gossiping] sorry—nae
thanks to her for the job—threw on my
hands mair than a year syne.   He's been
in Gartnavel since then, but in his wuts or
oot o' his wuts, which were but cat's wuts to
begin wi'——'

'You may keep a ceevil tongue in your
head,' said Tam indignantly ; ' you have not
sic a grip o' your ain wuts that you should
cast in his teeth that his have been to seek
since yours came back to you.'

'No offence,' said Sandy, showing the
example.   'But if you only kenned, your
honour, how I'm tried with the vermin—
you may glower [stare] but he's no better
—you would not fash for his feelin's.   He
has nae feelin's that I can find, and he does

not follow a word I say, unless it be about the ae blether that's gotten into the daft pow [head] o' him.'

It appeared as if Sandy were right, for not a trace of consciousness of the unceremonious remarks made upon him crossed the ugly, foxy, yet vacant face—from which almost every gleam of anything higher than the cunning of an animal had disappeared. Tam Drysdale glanced at the man with a mixture of pity and repugnance.

'What can I do?' asked Tam, in perplexity. 'Why hae you brought the miserable chiel to me?'

'Weel, the long and the short of it is, that in his wuts or out of his wuts, as I was sayin', he has gone on maunderin' [droning] about Drysdale Haugh, in connection with ane Mackinnon.'

'Stay!' said auld Tam; 'where did I hear some story of the kind? I mind now; and it was about a man in Gartnavel, too.'

'A' richt, sir. But see how the wild een

o' the cratur are lichtin' up, an' he's clutchin'
at the kistie under his oxter [arm]. So
long as he was in Gartnavel he micht
maunder as he liked; it would a' gang to
the general account—nobody would listen
to the drivel; but now that he's discharged
cured—a fell-like cure, when he's ten times
sillier than before—I thocht it behoved me
to communicate wi' you or Captain Mackinnon. It micht concern a gentleman's
credit to give the laddie a hearing—though
it is only some havers about seeing—selling
would be liker the word—a wheen [few] auld
papers he brocht with him frae the Hielants.
He never trusted me wi' them, though I've
been the best friend he has had for mony a
day. It was not with his wull that the
boxie was left with me when he was taken
to the asylum. They are not muckle worth
whatever, not as if there had been a gude
dug-cure or a famous mash for horses
among them: spun-out marriage lines and
a wull forty or fifty years back—that's the

head and tail of them, I believe,' ended
Sandy, with considerable scorn, betraying as
he spoke a suspicious familiarity with the
contents of the knapsack which had been
committed to his keeping.

Rory of the Shelties made his voice be
heard at last, with the startling effect of a
Brutus giving forth the sentiments of a man.

' The papers are mine,' he said with shrill
assertion. ' They were given to me by auld
Morag, her ain grannie, and she told me
to take care of them, and I have taken
care—there might be a fortune in them,
and the fortune is mine, every penny. Make
an offer, Mackinnon of Drysdale Haugh,'
and be quick aboot it, for I've been heckled
[cross-examined] and hunted, and shut up
in a prison. I'm thinkin' long of the Islands,
and I want to see the last of that big
brute Macnab.'

'Oh, the ungrateful demented blackgaird!'
cried Sandy, in righteous wrath. 'I can
hardly keep my hands aff him.'

Tam interposed, speaking severely.

'It would hae better become a reasonable being, and been a greater kindness to your afflicted countryman, to have seen him on board one of the Hielant boats, where he could have begged his passage north. 'My man,' turning soothingly to Rory, 'there is no person of the name and style you mention here. Drysdale Haugh is mine, but I'm not a Mackinnon. The son of the Mackinnon you seem to be seekin'— the father has been dead for more than a score of years—is an offisher lad at the Barracks; but he has nothing to do with Drysdale Haugh,' explained Tam with decision, 'as I have nothing to do with the Mackinnons; however, you may seek him out and hear what he says.'

'It was Mackinnon of Drysdale Haugh that auld Morag kenned,' persisted Rory doggedly. 'She gave me the names, and I'll stick to them.'

'You may stick to what you like, but

I'm afraid it cannot be here.' Auld Tam began to lose his patience.

'Ane of the papers is about a Drysdale, though,' said Sandy, unblushingly revealing more unaccounted-for knowledge. 'That is the reason I lugget the sinner here, and no to the Barracks ; but for that matter we need not have gone so far, since Captain Mackinnon's that thrang [intimate] with our young gentleman he's seldom awa' frae Semple Barns.'

'The deil thank you for as officious a scoondrel as he is a doited [stupid] ane,' thought Tam ; but he said aloud, with some alacrity—'Let's see the Drysdale paper. It may have reference to the auld master here. If so, I have a better right to it than any Mackinnon of them.'

'Open your wallet, Rory !' commanded Sandy Macnab.

'Mak' an offer, Mackinnon !' yelled Rory.

'Hout ! you thrawn taed [toad] , I doubt it's ill-gotten gear at the best. What call

have you to mak' terms, affrontin' me and
tantaleezin' a gentleman ?' and without
further preamble Sandy made a spring upon
the feeble defender of his property, pinned
him to his seat with one hand, and with the
other snatched the old knapsack, which fell
on the floor, bursting open, and scattering
the papers which were its contents.

Rory bit, scratched, and spat like a wild
cat, but remained helpless in his assailant's
powerful grasp.

'Hooly [hold] , Macnab !' cried Tam, and
started up.

As he did so, the toe of his shoe turned
over one of the bones of contention, and
he saw and read the address, written in a
large imposing hand, still legible, though the
ink had faded, and there was the dirt of
an intervening generation on the card,
' Gavin Mackinnon, Esq., King's Arms Inn,
North Uist.'

CHAPTER XXIII.

THE CONTENTS OF THE KNAPSACK.

' COME, this must be seen to,' said Tam half reluctantly, half roughly, for he felt that though he might have to act in his character of magistrate, personally he had got enough of the Mackinnons. He had no inclination to mix himself up in what was the business of the fellow who was Clary's foolish fancy, whom her father had begun to regard as his natural enemy. The probabilities flashed upon Tam as he reflected for an instant: ' Gavin Mackinnon was a great stravaiger [wanderer] after sport. He may have carried that article with a change of linen; he was a particular man in his dress, forgettin' what else had been stowed awa' in the bag, and then left it behind him. It was like the pompous, careless puppy; and now it has fallen to my lot to claim the papers in the name of their proper owner, if, indeed, one of them be not my ain concern.'

Opposite Tam, Sandy Macnab was still holding back his man, and enjoining him to 'bide still for a senseless dug,' or he might be had up for contempt of a magistrate, and committed as a vagrant and thief. The asylum was one thing and the county gaol another, as Rory might find to his cost.

Tam Drysdale, in search of a further clue, picked up a loose single sheet of paper which looked as if it had been wrapped round the other papers. It had a line or two written on it in the clear round text which belonged to the parish school of former days: 'Left behind by a Lowland gentleman, whose name appears to have been Gavin Mackinnon, but whose further address is unknown at the

King's Arms Inn, North Uist. It is probable that the property, which may be of value to the owner, will be called for.' Then followed a date of a quarter of a century back.

Whether the Morag who had been the grandmother of Rory, and had in course of time passed on to him the lost luggage, was a managing kinswoman of the innkeeper retired from business, or an acquisitive elderly chambermaid picking up what she could find —stowing it away in case it should come handy to herself at some future day, and ending by brooding on the unacknowledged possession till she hugely magnified its importance—Rory was never likely to tell, and there was no other person to explain.

'I cannot say that I approve of your mode of conductin' business, Sandy Macnab,' said Tam sternly. ' You may be taken up for assault if you do not take care. I would bid you let go your grip this minute, if you had to do with a reasonable being ; as it is, it will be on your head if you treat him like a cowardly brute when you see him off the premises, which I must ask you to do. I'll keep the papers. So far as I can judge, they are of little moment to anybody—which you've seen already, I doubt not. But whether that cratur is a born natural, or a raging madman, he has nothing to do with auld deeds—on the face of them.' As he spoke, Tam picked up two separate folded-up sheets of yellowing parchment. ' They must not be left in his hands. Stay! he seems to have been deluded into the belief that they were worth money, which he would receive when he delivered them up in the proper quarter. He had no warrant what-ever for detaining them; but as I under-stand he travelled south with them, to his ain loss of time and trouble, he may be entitled morally, if not legally, to some sma' compensation.'

' That's just what I've been thinking, Mr. Drysdale,' chimed in Sandy, glib and un-abashed, as Rory of the Shelties, exhausted

by the fruitless conflict, leant back panting
and glaring in the clutch of the other son of
the Gael. 'I kenned fine the scartipikin
[scarecrow] had neither airt nor pairt in the
papers in the kistie that he was so full o'.
But he cam' with them sooth, there can be
nae question of that; so I brocht him here to
deliver up his booty with his ain hands, and
get what reward or punishment was his due.'

'There's a five-pound note—and mind,
Macnab, you're answerable for what becomes
o't,' said Tam, handing over the money, at
which Rory, making a desperate effort,
caught with his bony fingers.

'Is it gude paper?' he demanded breath-
lessly; 'will it buy back Morag's cruivie
[croft]?'

'Hoots! ye maunna back-spear [cross-
question] a gentleman, or look a gift-
horse in the mooth; ye've come off
real weel when you micht be laid up in
jile for keepin' back papers that's no
your ain,' Sandy assured his compatriot

cheerfully. 'Out with your leather pouch, you ill-bred deil's buckie [devil's shell], and thank his honour—it's little thanks ye gie a body—and come your wa's without mair trouble; I'm sure ye've gien a hantle mair, since I kenned you first, than you're a' worth.'

'There's a couple of half-crowns to you, Sandy Macnab,' said Tam, on second thoughts. 'I believe you've not done so ill by this poor wretch. It would be well, if consistent with your duty to Sir Jeames, that you should see him on board ane of the Hielant boats before his pockets are picked and he's left to die on the streets.'

'Mony thanks—I'm your man, Mr. Drysdale. I'll be in Glasgy for mair medicine for the pups, that have ta'en the distemper, the day after the morn at farrest. I'll put the body into the hands of Nicol MacNicol, a steward, who is a friend of mine that gangs as far as the Lewis. Gude-day, sir!' and Sandy marched off with his unruly *protégé*.

Tam was left alone to inspect the papers which had come by a curious chance into his possession. The first, which Sandy had called 'spun-out marriage lines,' was, as Tam had taken for granted, the very marriage contract, the disappearance of which had been such a puzzle to the Miss Mackinnons. It was the deed drawn up jointly by David Milne and William Dalgleish, according to which Gavin Mackinnon and Margaret Craig had agreed that her property should be settled upon her. All that Tam Drysdale knew was that she set the agreement aside, by granting her husband and his partner power to sell both land and works, when Tam bought them for an old song, compared to what they would fetch now. The bargain had been made a year or two before Mrs. Mackinnon died, like her mother, in giving birth to her only child, the same supercilious 'offisher lad' who had become a thorn in Tam's flesh.

Tam regarded the deed as so much waste-paper, and merely glanced at it to see that he had been right in his conjecture of its purport. He had little sentiment to spare for the different circumstances in which it had been executed. He had never associated much feeling with Gavin Mackinnon and his wife, who had not, indeed, been sentimental persons. All that Tam Drysdale thought, as he folded up the document, was—

'Weel, Gauvin Mackinnon was never crouse [self-satisfied] when I kenned him; he had not the spunk [spirit] in him to be crouse, though he could blaw and give himself airs in his slow, lazy way. But if he ever were crouse, it must have been the nicht he signed that paper, and, without a penny belongin' to him, prepared to marry the heiress of Drysdale Haugh, and give her back her ain with a swagger, while he set himself to mismanage for her, and play ducks and drakes with her gudes. Puir woman! she had the worst of the bargain.

The son—confoond him for a fine gentleman of an offisher, who disdains to put
himself forrit!—seems up to the same trick,
as auld as the hills and as shabby as a worn
saxpence. Before I sorned [lived] on ony
woman I would cast aff my coat and break
stanes at the side of the road. But he'll
not get in his hand if I can help it—not
though Clary were so far left to hersel'—a
lassie with Clary's wit! But in that case
he'll tak' her as she stands, she'll not get a
farthing of mine; she can follow the drum
if that be her will, only young Tam, who
may need the sillar, and little Eppie, who
would never cross her father, will be the
gainers. But it cannot be; Clary's not a
fule, though she's high-headed, to fling
hersel' awa' on a great pithless lump—just
because he has the richt to put on the
Queen's regimentals, which, nowadays, neither he nor his brother offishers have the
speerit to wear, and is made welcome to
straik [stretch] his lang legs beneath sic a

table as that at Semple Barns. No, it canna be.'

It was an annoyance to Tam that he should be burdened, even to the small extent of having to keep this old marriage contract, till he could hand it over to the person for whom he had so little esteem, who had the best right to it. Tam might be safely depended upon to take prompt steps to ascertain whether young Mackinnon was at Semple Barns, where he stayed so often, or when he was expected there, in order to get rid of the trust.

Tam Drysdale turned with much more interest to what proved the will of his namesake, the original owner of the Drysdale Haugh farm and works. The two papers had no doubt been brought together at the time of the drawing out of the marriage contract, in the office of one or other of the lawyers, and had eventually been lost in company by Gavin Mackinnon's notorious incompetence.

The loss need not have been hopeless, if the Miss Mackinnons had but known it. Copies of the deeds would have been found in the proper places. But small blame to Miss Janet for her ignorance, since Tam Drysdale—a good business man, for whom the law had a certain fascination—shared her lack of information on these points.

Tam examined the will carefully, but without much speculation how it had come there, and whether it was the sole indica-tion of the dead man's pleasure in the disposal of his property. He had no reason to doubt what had been his father's cousin's meaning, and it would have taken a power-ful reason to shake his broad acquiescence in all that had happened. If he read the settlement slowly, every word, it was from a motive quite apart from any eager desire or vague impulse to dispute its authority. Early associations were rising thick and fast, and filling his mind. He recalled the old man, homely and a little harsh, but not unrighteous or altogether untender, when his mother had sometimes received permission to take her boy to the farm-house. He had not been without little re-lentings and kindnesses to Tam and his mother, though he had openly and in-dignantly condemned the husband and father who had wasted his little patrimony and sunk to the lowest social grade, dragging down his wife and child in the process. Neither had old Drysdale ever concealed his intention of leaving his goods past his Drys-dale cousins to his late wife's niece, Mrs. Craig, in India. He had talked openly of the arrangement as one he had entered into when he took home the lass-bairn and fancied she would be the solace of his old age. He had been mistaken, but he had made the stipulation, and it was not for him to break his part of the bargain, while the poor, credulous lass, who must drink as she had brewed, might want all the help that he could give her. It was for

young Tam—auld Tam was young Tam in
these days—who was a brisk, sturdy laddie,
to work, to redeem what his father had
lost. It was the discipline which might
save the son from going the same road;
for anything else—such as gifting the chap
who had begun the world a working lad
with gear he had never earned—would
have been in these austere eyes to send
him straight to destruction.

And Tam had never greatly grudged the
alienation of the property, for which he had
always been prepared, though the moment
he had seen the possibility he had worked
hard to recover it. But it gave him a
thrill now, though he was not a super-
stitious man, to handle and study the
document, as nearly as possible on the spot
where it had been devised. He could
conjure up the circumstances—the old man
sitting solitary, but without visible weakness, nay, stiff, upright, and determined,
in his bare parlour; the complacent lawyer

from the town waiting his instructions; a tolerable bottle of wine—not the sour stuff the Miss Mackinnons treasured, but good wine of its kind, ordered for the old man's infirmities—or two rummers of toddy and a plate with a cut lemon standing between the couple.

Tam remembered to have heard a characteristic anecdote of his namesake's scorn of insincerity and of covert acts to obtain by favour what had not been justified by right, or by work done for the coveted reward.

The old man had taken it into his head that his doctor, in addition to his claim for the fee of which he was certain, had surreptitious views on the sick man's estate, and desired to figure as a legatee in his will. On the last night that the medical man visited his patient, whose hours were numbered, the undaunted invalid suddenly asked for the physician's cane, which was furnished with a cord and tassel. The sick man, amidst the wondering, half-scared looks of the watchers, raised himself in bed and asked for a penknife and a bit of narrow black riband which happened to be lying near. With feeble hands he cut away the cord and tassel, laced the riband through the hole in the wood, tied it in a little bow, and then handed the stick back to its owner, with a formal inclination of the head, saying: 'There, sir, are both your murnins and your legacy.' Within a few hours from perpetrating the grim jest, the jester departed this life.

Tam wondered what his kinsman would have thought if he could have seen the result of his will. Surely he must have approved and been proud of the achievements of his descendant. Tam straightened himself, got up and took a turn across his business-room with something of the peacock strut which, alas! sometimes distinguished him. He thought of the greatly enlarged and improved works, the im-

mensely extended trade, the honour in the
commercial world, the field added to field,
the grand house, the friendship of such
men as Sir James and Sir Hugo Willoughby,
the position of Tam's family when it had
been thought that little Eppie might end
by being 'my leddy,' and contrasted all
these changes with the limited and clumsy
materials of the past, the small reputation,
the plain farmhouse, and its almost sordid
domestic economy.

Blood was thicker than water. Though
Tam's cousin had once on a day been fond
as a father of his dead wife's niece, the
girl he had brought up, she had disappointed him, and he had never got over
his rooted dislike to Jock Craig. Old Drysdale had not so much as made mention of
any children of the marriage in dictating
the deed. It was but an accident, after
all, the fact that Mrs. Craig had survived
her uncle by a few hours, which had stood
between Tam's father, despised reprobate as

he had been, and the inheritance of Drysdale Haugh.

Tam himself had never before fully realized how close the run had been, how narrow the escape of Mrs. Craig's infant daughter from the forfeiture of her mother's succession. It would have made a difference. He would have been saved from a youth of toil and hardship, for he would very soon have come into his father's shoes.

The poor prodigal from whom Tam had drawn his being, though his physique was from his mother, had been near his last gasp when fortune dealt him the final blow, which none could say had been undeserved. Not even the strong stimulant of unexpected good fortune would have prolonged his life for many months, or given him time to squander the larger inheritance as he had squandered the smaller. Tam would have come into it almost intact. He might have been able to educate himself while he

was yet young, to spare himself many a
drudging day and weary night.

But looking back calmly over the gulf
of years, with the mountains of difficulty
well past, the man decided it was better as
it had been. He had profited by the war-
fare he had undergone—it had made twice
the man of him that he might have been
otherwise. It was more honourable to have
hewed out the fortune which he honestly
thought so great and enviable, than to have
derived even a part of it from the gift of
another. Tam held his head the higher
for the thought. At the same time he
would not return the will which had so
strangely found its way to him unsought,
till he saw a clear obligation to relinquish
it. Surely it was more his property than
that of any Mackinnon of them, whose
name did not even occur in its pages.
When it came to the question, it was not
probable that anybody, be he a Mackinnon
or a stranger, would wrangle with Tam for

the possession of an old deed which had taken effect and been overturned by Tam's own purchase, more than twenty years before.

With regard to the marriage contract, it was clearly young Mackinnon's. But the next day Tam ascertained that Mr. Mackinnon was not at Semple Barns, and that he was not expected there soon, for the good reason that he and Dick Semple had gone in a friend's yacht to Norway. Their present address was unattainable, and by the time they returned, the Drysdales would have gone with the rest of the world to the coast. The matter was of little consequence. Any unnecessary intercourse between Tam and the young man, while Tam's feelings towards him were what has been stated, would be, to say the least, the reverse of agreeable. The matter might stand over. The paper was safer in Tam's desk than it had been for many a day. Altogether it seemed the natural and proper

course to wait till the two men came in
contact again, in the ordinary intercourse,
at Semple Barns or elsewhere, before telling
the story and committing Guy Mackinnon's
marriage contract to the keeping of his
son.

CHAPTER XXIV.

THE DEATH OF FENTON OF STRATHDIVIE.

It was the height of summer, when the most of the inhabitants of Glasgow and its neighbourhood, who had the opportunity, had taken refuge by the water, which is, somehow, the natural element of every true Glaswegian, man or woman, high or low.

The Drysdales were at Lochgoilhead, the Semples of Semple Barns at Oban. Dr. Peter Murray had got a medical substitute to take his post for a fortnight, and was spending the minister's holiday to his heart's content with Athole, scrambling after ferns and sea-anemones in Arran. Young Eppie was wearing her Newhaven fishwife's costume, and looking the loveliest and daintiest little fishwife that ever trod an Arcadian shore. She was learning to spout 'Lord Ullin's Daughter,' without much anxiety as to whether Loch Goyle could be the same 'dark and stormy water' which Campbell meant. But there was no Sir Hugo to gaze on the nymph and hang on the accents of the Clydesdale tongue. He had not yet turned up in the course of the Long Vacation. Guy Horsburgh alleged that his friend could not help himself—his heart was in the right place—that is, in Glasgow and its dependencies; but his tutor and his mother had set their hearts on his completing his college course with some credit, and to do so he must give a few weeks to a certain reading-party, which meant work, in Derbyshire. But Derbyshire, or any other shire in the United Kingdom, was little more than a bow-shot off, from which, when he had made the necessary sacrifice, Sir Hugo was certain to present himself

within the given number of hours. That
might or might not be. There are plenty
of allurements for such golden lads as Sir
Hugo.

A little fickleness may be excused in
them, especially when they are hardly more
than major. Some rumour of threatened
danger might have reached his friends.
They might have taken the alarm, and be
moving heaven and earth successfully to
keep him in their own circle. If it were
so, nobody would object, as Tam Drysdale
had said; and least of all young Eppie,
who had done all but forget that such a
grand young gentleman as an English
baronet had ever crossed her blithe path,
caught her unawares, caused her to think
shame, and made up for it by being good-
natured in admiring her singing. Eppie
was as happy as usual—as happy as the
day was long. She was still at the most
joyous age—fancy-free and untouched by
care. None missed a recreant lover, whether

by compulsion or his own free will, less than she did.

For inevitably there were more defaulters than Sir Hugo. Lochgoilhead, Arran, and Oban may not look far apart on the map, and in the summer season steamboats churn the water of the river continually with so little pause and stay, that the throb of the engines, the grey and white wreaths of the smoke and steam, the foam-bells on the track, are never absent, any more than the near and far shadows of the hills from the landscape. To think of getting out of sight and sound of these harbingers of universal movement, is to imagine that one can sit on certain green lawns, and count a dozen without catching a glimpse of a white butterfly specking the sunny blue air. Still Lochgoilhead, Arran, and Oban are too far apart for the exchange of morning or evening calls. The 'runs' of the steamboats do not always answer particular requirements, but keep crossing each other and cutting off the dwellers on one point of the mainland or on one island from the dwellers on another, in the most perplexing and exasperating manner. In truth, the service of steamboats is kept for families coming once for all and taking up their summer quarters, with periodical returns to the city, or for tourists and touring, not for visitors and visiting. These last social features are reserved for settled life in town or country-houses—not nomadic life on the coast. When, in addition to this reservation, some men have business engagements, such as young Tam had, only letting them out of Glasgow at the last moment, once or twice a week, with an obligation to report themselves first to their own people; or when officers have regimental duty, such as was binding on Eneas Mackinnon; and when there are not frank, hospitable invitations sent beforehand for gay bachelors to come down in the end of the week and stay over Sunday in Arran or at Lochgoil-

head, the most ardent lover may be safely
defied to dance attendance on the object of
his affections.

And young Tam was not ardent in
pursuing a perverse young woman who was
constantly fleeing from him and mocking
him. He had his wayward moods like hers;
often he set his teeth and said he would
have nothing more to do with her, that
he despised himself for going after her; not
that he meant anything by it—oh no!   It
was merely regard for Dr. Peter and a determination not to be driven away by her
snubs and laughter.

Eneas Mackinnon was not ardent in a
hopeless chase which he felt was madness.
He made up his mind half-a-dozen times a
day to withdraw even from the passive
attentions and silent love-making which
were all he could presume to offer. But
on every occasion that Claribel sailed across
his path, he was drawn by the fascination
of her strength and sufficiency for what

she cared for, as much as by her beauty, to break his resolution and let himself be dashed afresh against the rocks of fortune.

Altogether Clary and Athole, who had never confided in each other, never consulted together, who found themselves two young women abandoned largely to their own company, or the society of their nearest relations, needed all Clary's *sang froid* and Athole's gaiety of heart and devotion to her father, to bear their desertion with anything like the unaffected philosophy and cheerfulness which young Eppie displayed in similar circumstances.

The young ladies paid for their superior rank and refinement, and had less of good fellowship during their holiday than their sisters in the grade beneath them. These lower middle-class girls, not coy or capricious, managed to secure their brief spell of liberty from their situations as nursery governesses, in shops, and milliners' establishments, at the same time that the young clerks and shopmen, in their train, obtained their breathing-space. All rushed down, with the other members of their families, to Hunter's Quay, or Sandbank, or Kirn, and were never apart. These primitive young people spent the long summer day till far on in the dusk of the summer night, mostly on the water, in such jovial play—such chattering, singing, laughing, flirting, quarrelling, and agreeing again, as made the very hills of Cowal ring, and formed enough recreation to last through all the working-hours, till the depths of winter, and the daft days—stretching from Hogmanay to Handsel Monday—came again.

There were multitudes, however, who never quitted the dingy precincts of the city. Among these were the Miss Mackinnons. Dr. Peter and Athole had done their best, in vain, to persuade the sisters to go out and keep house at Barley Riggs, in the absence of the owners, as a favour to them. But no invitation to Drysdale Hall had come to the old ladies this year. The omission had drawn forth sundry expressions of surprise from Dr. Peter; and when Athole had hinted at an explanation, he had stared, reddened, and said plainly it was a shabby piece of retaliation, such as he would not easily have believed Tam Drysdale guilty of.

Then Athole pointed out that she was aware the Drysdale Hall baskets of fruit, vegetables, and dairy produce continued to come, as they had done for a year, to St. Mungo's Square; but Miss Janet began to look dubiously at them, and to ask sharply if there was no card or note among the contents. On this second piece of information, Dr. Peter shook his head, and remarked emphatically *that* would not do.

The Miss Mackinnons' excuse for not going out of Glasgow was that Miss Mackinnon was so frail, she was better at home. It had become a 'thought' to take her even the short distance to Barley Riggs in a close carriage.

But in place of remaining quiet and composed, like fixtures, in their own house, there was an air of restlessness and expectation about the sisters, from the youngest to the eldest. It could hardly be accounted for by the fact which Miss Bethia had disclosed to Athole Murray. The elder lady had said, with a wistful, frightened look in her eyes, that ill news travelled fast, and they were not easy in their minds about a friend who had been long ailing and was likely to leave them this summer.

Sure enough, the Miss Mackinnons had learnt from some quarter that Fenton of Strathdivie, after many a false alarm, was on his death-bed at last.

The expectant heirs did not speak much to each other of what they had been looking forward to all these years, of what was never out of their thoughts. The Miss Mackinnons were simple women when it comes to that. The subject was too awful —too ghastly—the feverish counting of the

failing sands of a human creature's existence in this world, the breathless waiting
till his breath went out, by women—two
of them considerably older than the sufferer
—that they might join together in parting
their portion of the dead man's possessions,
was not an experience to be lightly alluded
to.

Miss Janet would say abruptly there was
' a het glaff [warm air] off the plain-stanes.'
Such warm weather must be very trying—
even in the country, where there were grass
and cornfields—to sick folk, who could not
be expected to stand its exhausting effects.

Miss Bethia would reply below her breath
to the vague allusion—'I wonder how *he* is;
sair spent, puir man, I doubt not.'

And Miss Mackinnon, narrowly watching her sister's eyes, would hastily utter
the imperious appeal, ' Have you heard
word ?'

For weeks Miss Janet or Miss Bethia had
anticipated the coming of the postman on

his morning rounds. One or other of the sisters had stolen out when the ringing of the door-bells grew nearer, and been found on the door-step as the man of letters approached, waved a polite but indifferent negative, and passed on in his circuit of the Square, chuckling to himself when his back was turned, and saying, ' The auld lasses' day for love-letters is surely gone by.'

It was in the forenoon, however, that Miss Bethia, returning from marketing, and not noticing any change on the outside of the house, stumbled as she entered out of the broad sunshine with which the opened front door had flooded the hall, into the dining-room, where all the blinds were drawn down. She stopped on the threshold with a mingled shiver and thrill, as she saw through the gloom Miss Janet, sitting erect and pale, opposite Miss Mackinnon, who was crouching a little, as if from cold, on a summer day, while on the table between them lay two black-edged letters unopened.

'We are waiting for you, Betheye,' said
Miss Janet solemnly.

'Oh, gie me a minute, Janet,' implored
Miss Bethia, dropping into a chair, and
speaking as if her own execution were approaching. 'When did it happen? What
is the upshot? I hope none of us will
fent. Had we not better have burnt
feather and smelling-salts in readiness?'

'And the doctor, and the minister—I was
gaun to say the lawyer, but we have not had
a man of business for the last twal years,'
said Miss Janet, provoked to sarcasm.
'You were aye a frichted hen, Betheye;
but we're not of the fentin' kind. As to
what has happened, and the upshot, I'm
gaun to see. I take it for granted that I
hae baith your permissions.'

And with that Miss Janet stretched forward a wrinkled hand, that only shook
slightly, and appropriated the letters.

The first was a mere intimation of the
death.

'Strathdivie, 15th July.

'Mr. Archibald Fenton died here this morning at half-past three o'clock.'

Miss Janet read the announcement without faltering, then handed the card for Miss Mackinnon's satisfaction.

'Eh! sirs!' exclaimed Miss Bethia, by way of decent lamentation. 'Eh! sirs!' she repeated after a moment's pause, not without a little guilty consciousness of hypocrisy. 'The news will take nobody by surprise. He suffered a deal of sickness, poor felly, but now he's at his rest.' It was a statement, not a prayer, yet the assertion, in a softened tone, was somewhat equivalent to the Roman Catholics' petition, '*Requiescat in pace.*'

Miss Janet was already opening the second letter, and drawing herself up when she saw it was from a lawyer's office; but, as a matter of course, the only fresh intelligence it conveyed, in addition to communicating the fact of Fenton of Strathdivie's death, in slightly different words, amounted to no more than that the funeral was to be from Strathdivie on the following Thursday, and that the reading of the will would take place on the return of the mourners from the churchyard.

' That means that we are invited to attend as interested parties,' said Miss Janet, in a tone of triumph, forgetting the melancholy occasion of the invitation.

' What will we do ?' asked Miss Bethia helplessly, fanning herself with a corner of her pocket-handkerchief, and feeling instinctively as she did so the impropriety of its not being broad-hemmed.

' What will we do ? We'll gang, of course,' said Miss Janet, both asking a question and answering it with the utmost decision. ' We're no daft to hang back and decline to claim our legacy, that was left to us in the first place by our great-grandfather when his dochter Jean took her tocher to Fenton of Strathdivie.'

'But how can we gang?' retorted Miss Bethia, in her matter-of-factness, still full of doubts and difficulties.

'On our feet and in the trains to be sure,' said Miss Janet impatiently.

'But the murnins.'

'You cannot have forgotten, Betheye,' Miss Janet reminded her sister severely, 'that every stitch we've bocht for the last four years has been black, in expectation of this ca'? As for crape and weepers, we'll surely get credit for them till the will's administered.'

'Oh, Janet, you're makin' cock-sure,' said Miss Bethia in a timorous voice, oddly at variance with the masculine word she had used.

'And what for no?' demanded Miss Janet, with all her old audacious spirit. 'Are we not come of the blude of our ain great-grandfather? Did not his dochter Jean marry Fenton of Strathdivie? and failin' the Fentons, was not a share of

Strathdivie cleared from debt by her portion
to come back to the Mackinnons ?   It's as
plain as a pikestaff.'

'And what are we to do with Meye ?'
Miss Bethia started another obstacle.

'You may ask hersel',' suggested Miss
Janet, still with unshaken confidence.   'I
think I ken her answer beforehand.'

'Meye,' Miss Janet wrote, 'I say we
should start the morn for Strathdivie—what
do you think ?'

'I'll go,' replied Miss Mackinnon, without a second's hesitation.

'Hear to her, Betheye,' said Miss Janet,
with a mixture of pride and reproach, 'and
her weel up among her seventies, and as
deaf as a door-nail, and has not had a
breath of wind blow on her this year.   Are
you not ashamed of yoursel' ?'

'I would do onything,' said Miss Bethia
meekly; 'but should we not wait for the
Lieutenant ?   It is his business as well as
ours.   He micht gang in our stead; or if

that would not serve, he micht be our con-
voy and protection.'

' We'll wait nane,' said Miss Janet, in her
high-handed way. ' How are we to write
and hear word back again in time from Oban ?
He was not to be at the Barracks for a week.
If we do not gang when we're bidden, how
do we ken that some other claimant may not
slip into our shoon? Legacies do not go
a-begging. There will be plenty of corbies
and gleds [ravens and kites] to pike for
Fenton of Strathdivie's leavin's.'

' That's the very reason we should be
careful,' said Miss Bethia eagerly, ' not to
rin into terrible expense without assurance.'

' What do you ca' assurance, Betheye
Mackinnon ? You may do what you like,
but for mysel' I ken I do not come into an
inheritance ilka day. I would go to Strathdivie though I were to walk berfit [bare-
footed] every step of the gate, though I
were to beg my way from farm-toon to
farm-toon. You'll say next that we have

not waited long, and that we have no need
o' the siller.' She ended almost fiercely in
her exasperation. Then she began again :
' I believe you're feared like a bairn—you're
fingie [coward] enough of travellin' to a
house where a coffin and a corp' are lyin'—
a woman of your years! As if they could
harm you ; as if our presence were not the
last mark of respect to him that's awa';
as if, gin he were to hant us, he couldna as
lief come here as gang yonder—here, where
we're bund to admit his wa'ga'in' [depar-
ture] has been sair wearied for.'

' Oh! Janet, haud your tongue, for
mercy's sake, and let us do what you judge
best ! I never wanted to gang conter to
you,' cried Miss Bethia, collapsing utterly
before these scornful reproaches and grue-
some threats.

Accordingly the Miss Mackinnons prepared for an extraordinary exodus on the
following day. First, they set their house
in order, toiling for the next six hours,

putting aside and locking up everything that could be locked up, and packing a trunk in common. They found an old washer-woman, and placed her in charge of the bare walls and the tables and chairs, loading her with instructions for the careful preservation of other people's property. Not content with this, the old ladies charged the policeman on the beat, the postman, and a mechanic they knew, who crossed St. Mungo's Square as he went to and from his day's work, to have an eye on Jenny in her employers' interests.

Then, giddy with excitement, and all but spent with fatigue, the indefatigable old women turned again to the packing of the common trunk. Miss Bethia especially brought to it all manner of incongruous articles of apparel that would have filled half a dozen trunks. She excused herself for this bulky plaid, or that old gown or bonnet, which had not been seen for years, on the plea that the travellers could not tell how long they would stay. Strathdivie was in a moorland district, and they might feel the change of climate in the country; and while it was necessary to prepare for seeing company, particularly at a time like this, ladies might also wear up such old dresses as their owners could not appear in so long as they remained in town.

It was well that exhaustion brought some amount of sleep, though the sleepers' dreams could not but have been uncanny.

By dawn of day the whole party were again astir, preparing to start for the railway station an hour before the train was due. Miss Janet, who had all the practical ability that was now to be found among the sisters, had borrowed a time-table and copied out the stages of the journey.

A certain sense of awe, very different from any former experience on leaving home, was lent to the departure, from the indefinite duration of the stay at Strathdivie—together with what were to the women the

tremendous issues involved in the visit.
The starting took place early in the morning, before even Miss Janet's and Miss
Bethia's time of rising. It was as if they
were fleeing, unknown to the sleepers around
them, from the long reign of poverty and
privation by which they had been well-
nigh overborne, as if the news were too
good to be true, and something terrible
must befall the maiden ladies on their
strange journey to the house of the dead.
He had never invited them to be his guests
during his lifetime—he had, indeed, as was
shrewdly suspected, nourished a strong, not
unnatural, prejudice against those Mackinnons he had known. It was, Miss
Bethia said to herself with a sob in her
throat, as if they might never come back to
the house in which they had been born,
where they had dwelt from youth to age,
which they had never failed to honour. It
was dear to them from many causes—from
their intimate familiarity with every flower

on the wall-papers, every crack in the ceilings—from such joys as had come to them —from the sufferings they had bravely faced under its roof. It was their own house and their father's house, which they were to bequeath to Eneas.

Miss Janet's daring expenditure had not reached the pitch of calling a cab. The grey morning was only mildly threatening rain, as it so often does in the humid west, and had not settled down into steady wet. St. Mungo's Square was not above ten minutes' walk from the particular railway station where there were trains which led, by several changes and a corresponding number of halts, to within a quarter of a mile of Strathdivie.

The ladies went on foot, Miss Janet giving her arm to Miss Mackinnon, and a porter—by whom Miss Bethia was appointed to walk that she might keep her eye upon him without a moment's intermission—shouldering the trunk.

Emile Souvestre in one of his tales has an account of two sisters who had led a peculiarly simple and retired life, having been, from the force of circumstances, kept not only in drudgery, but in tutelage, till they were far advanced in middle age. Then they were suddenly set free, and began doubtfully to look about them, and take the holidays which the women had missed in their youth. The graceful and not unsubtle French writer—whom it is the fashion to set aside, because of his modesty and purity, for the hurried perusal of heedless schoolgirls—describes with delicate touches and fine sympathy the tender pathos of the situation—the clinging helplessness of the pair who should long ago have been the helpers of others—the stammering timidity of the grey-headed women who ought by rights to have faced the world half a century before.

There was some parallel between this case and that of the Miss Mackinnons when they set out for Strathdivie in order to come into their kingdom. True, there was no trace of timidity where Miss Janet was concerned, and the explanation was rather that powers which had once existed had fallen into disuse, and former knowledge had become forgotten, than that the Scotch ladies had never gone abroad among their contemporaries, or mingled with the world on their own account. On the other hand, the nature of this errand, so different from the mere pursuit of pleasure late in the day by the French sisters, was, in itself, tragical and overpowering.

The three ladies had a look of blinking owls, as the Miss Mackinnons stood on the platform, keeping guard over their trunk, waiting for their train, while they interfered with the traffic, got in the way of the porters and other passengers, and were more than once heartily anathematized. Even Miss Janet made mistakes, dropped tickets, miscounted her money, and entered into hope-

less altercations, trotting backward and
forward as fast as her stiffened limbs would
let her, till she was thoroughly put out and
agitated.

When the group were seated in a third-
class carriage—for they were not yet in
possession of the reversion of Jean Mackinnon's tocher—various rough jests and not
too civil remarks were made by the by-
standers on 'the party out of the ark that
had ta'en the road, forgetting that they had
left Noehey behind them.' Happily the
jeering personalities fell as flat on Miss
Janet's and Miss Bethia's hearing ears, as
on the sealed organs of Miss Mackinnon,
seated between the two, for the better execution of any pantomime that might convey
to her what was passing beyond her range
of vision. The younger sisters never dreamt
that the talk applied to themselves.

'Wha are they speaking about, Janet?'
asked Miss Bethia calmly.

'Dear kens,' answered Miss Janet, with

the same coolness.   ' But I dinna heed; I've
a great deal to think about, Betheye.'

' Nae doubt, Janet,' and the subject
dropped.

The complete imperturbability of the
objects of the ridicule not only blunted the
words, it gradually shut the mouths of the
thoughtless mockers.

CHAPTER XXV.

STRATHDIVIE.

It was afternoon when the Miss Mackinnons were set down, sorely wearied, at the roadside station which was the nearest to Strathdivie. Happily, the day still kept ' up,' in country phrase ; but it was grey and still, as was the scantily-populated moorland country which the travellers had reached. They had left the black country round Glasgow behind them ; but they had come to a region which needed all the summer sunshine to render it cheerful—a peaty, boggy, clayey district—where land had been brought in from the waste with much labour that seemed wasted, for when all was done the grass looked sour and the corn dropsical.

Yet the prevailing colours of the landscape would have delighted an art student, since they hovered between the olive-brown of moss, the sombre green of rushes, and the blue-green of late oats in a sparse and un-thrifty condition. Brickfields with their clay hillocks and smoking kilns, rows on rows of half-dried bricks, and piles of broken and crumbling-down bricks, like ungainly masses of sordid ruins, were the most flourishing form of industry. Strathdivie was in sight, a discoloured, tall and narrow last-century house, reminding the gazer of a gaunt face foul with weeping, half hidden in a neglected fir-wood. Fenton of Strathdivie had not possessed spirit or ability, for long years back, to keep his surroundings trim and fair to see.

This was the paradise the Miss Mackinnons had sighed for. But the sight of it did not daunt them—at least not Miss Janet—more than a second.

'It is an auld-fashioned pairt, without

ony nonsense,' said that indomitable woman;
' and auld-fashioned farmin' aye paid. I
dare say these brickfields have been Archie
Fenton's—they say there's no such flourishin'
trade now as the buildin' trade, and that
there is a grand profit got out o' drain-tiles.
I wouldna wonder though he has doobled
his capital, and that there is plenty of
stouchrie [stowed away goods] in the auld
hoose.'

' He's had to leave it a',' said Miss Bethia,
mentioning the undeniable truth in a low,
grave tone, that sought instinctively to sub-
due the loud excited key, verging on exultation, in which Miss Janet spoke.

' Would you have had him tak' it wi'
him? I call that a very haythen notion,'
Miss Janet retorted successfully.

The most serious difficulty which presented
itself was that there had been a miscalcula-
tion of the strength of Miss Mackinnon.
She was trembling in every limb. Certainly
she could not walk even the short distance

to Strathdivie, if her journey to claim her legacy were not to prove her death. After an anxious consultation with the station-master, it was found that a cart with a straw-stuffed sack could be had from the small wayside inn opposite the station. In this primitive conveyance, sitting all three elevated on their uncomfortable perch, tired and faint, for they had long ago eaten the few biscuits they had brought to break their fast, the descendants of the Virginian Mackinnons drove up to the goal of their hopes.

The rough paddock, the neglected flower-border, the walled-in garden where the mossy wall was conspicuously broken and out of repair, the pigeon-house, which was tottering to its fall, so that no prudent pigeon would abide within its crazy shelter; the dead trees left within sight of the windows; the old, empty dog-kennel, adorned by a rusty chain, kicked over, and lying rotting in a damp corner, were unfashionable enough in their untidiness to please Miss Janet, and appeal to her enthusiasm ; but whether the tokens were those of sluttish plenty, or of narrowing means growing squalid in despair, remained to be proved.

Mr. Fenton had been without near relations, or, indeed, kindred in any degree, dwelling under his roof. He had been taken care of in his latter days by a couple of old servants —a man and his wife, who, in their very fidelity, looked with jealous suspicion on all invaders of the dead man's domains, where his retainers had long ruled paramount.

The woman, who was the housekeeper, in a black cap and plaid shawl, opened the door, that creaked inhospitably on its hinges, as if it had grown rusty from the rarity of its opening, in answer to the challenge of the Miss Mackinnons' young carter rudely rapping with his whip on one of the panels. He horrified his freight, who were not in time to stop him with the stern remonstrance, 'Man, are you forgetting there's death in the house?'—a reminder that he was disturbing the quiet of *that* within which was greater than the presence of kings, before which all must bow.

The housekeeper, with blinking eyes and a tightly closed mouth, offered a passive resistance to the strangers, though Miss Janet immediately recovered her confidence, and made a bold approach to the citadel. She announced herself and her sisters as the late Mr. Fenton's Glasgow cousins, who were come to Strathdivie as a matter of course, to be in the house when the master was carried out of it, and to 'take charge of things' after he was gone, in consideration of what was due both to him and to themselves.

Mrs. Todd, the housekeeper, stood there like stone, filling up the gap made by the half-open door, not yielding an inch to Miss Janet's intrepid advance, simply asking with sharp significance where was the ladies' authority for requiring her to admit them to her master's house ? She did not even say

her late master, thus acknowledging that
his rule, which he had delegated to her and
her husband, was an affair of the past, and
that others might now be entitled to lay
down the law where he had once given his
orders.   He must be fairly ' in the mools '
(earth) before such a reversal of matters
took place, and she would know the reason
why before she consented to it.

It seemed doubtful whether the Miss
Mackinnons could make good their entrance,
even after unseemly contention ; whether
they would not find the door shut in their
astounded faces, and the old travellers
turned back on the inhospitable wilds—
that is, thrown with their small purse on the
deficient accommodation of the station inn
—as Miss Janet would have said, 'Fell-like
quarters for maiden leddies !'

Fortunately this catastrophe was avoided.
There was already shut up in the most con-
venient room, with an open desk and a few
papers before him, an elderly experienced

country lawyer. He was well known to
Mrs. Todd, and had established his right to
be there. He had been Mr. Fenton's man
of business, and was appointed to conduct
the funeral. He was the same lawyer who
had written to the Miss Mackinnons with
the news of the death. Mrs. Todd obeyed
him all the more implicitly since, clever
woman though she was for her station and
opportunities, she had a vague idea that the
joint legacy which she counted on for herself
and her husband depended on ' the writer's'
goodwill.

Thus, when Mr. Mair, attracted to the
window by the rumble of wheels, bustled
out, introduced himself to the Miss Mackinnons, handed them from their cart, and
directed, with no lack of the necessary
authority, that they should be taken in and
made comfortable, Mrs. Todd submitted
with a decent show of civility. But all the
more because of the compulsion to change
her bearing, the enmity pretty sure to have

arisen between her and the new-comers
was established.

It was a restrained enmity as yet, however, even where Miss Janet was concerned.
She was a little subdued now that she had
come into the near neighbourhood of death,
and she and her sisters were too tired and
disturbed generally not to avail themselves
thankfully of the refreshment and rest afforded
them—however grudgingly. The plausible
writer-body was willing to receive them, and
that was a good sign. Who would mind a
sour servant? Auld bachelors like poor Archie
Fenton aye spoilt servants, who went
on trading upon former privileges.

It would have been well if the Miss Mackinnons had been troubled with no further
arrière pensées than belonged either to Mrs.
Todd's churlishness or her forced politeness.
The sisters were not imaginative women.
Their minds did not wander off to the days of
the dead man's youth and his high hope, to
the hour of his birth in that very house, where

his entrance into the world had doubtless been hailed with pride and joy, equal to the exultation with which they, his remote kins-women, had hailed the arrival among them of their grand-nephew, Eneas. They did not ask what had become of all the shattered dreams which had come into existence since then, and whether this lonely end were the fitting conclusion to the blithe beginning of more than threescore years before. The Miss Mackinnons would have said that they were Christian women, and it was the Lord's will ; and, if anything more was to be added, they trusted Archie Fenton had gone to ' a better place.'

Yet the sisters could not get rid of the wonder of what he who was lying motion-less within four oaken boards in the best bedroom would have thought of their being here in what had been his house. Mrs. Todd had not failed to point out a closed door, with grim attention, as the ladies passed with trembling feet and bated breath. 'That

is where the master is lying,' Mrs. Todd
had said. He was no longer master; still,
what would he have thought—nay, what
did he think now, if thought remained to
him? But surely he was in a position to
acknowledge their right when he had joined
the great company in which his and their
forbears mingled—among them that very
Jean Mackinnon who had brought her tocher
to Strathdivie, whose half-washed-out name
Miss Janet detected with an irrepressible
thrill of delight on the towel which she got
to dry her hands. Another member of that
company was Jean's father, the haughty
Virginian merchant that had made ' a' Glasgow trimle at the wag of his finger.' Well,
he might be in regions where men had ceased
to tremble before a fellow-creature. Still,
not even in another world could it be believed that he was wholly unmoved by the
fate of the descendants for whom he had
provided so carefully, looking forward, as it
had happened, ' well on for a hundred years.'

'Yes,' Miss Janet assented fervently, glancing round on the coarse, clumsy, and shabby, rather than quaintly grotesque, antiquely-solid or richly-wrought furniture —on the faded out-of-date drugget protecting the hideous red and green carpets—the blackened portraits of gaunt or plethoric, hard or heavy-featured men and women on the wall—on the absence of all that was fresh, bright, open-minded, and cheerful. Strathdivie was all her fancy had painted it, and it was like coming to another home to be there. She wrote her sensations to Miss Mackinnon, who responded to them, though with less effusion.

Nevertheless, it was a somewhat ghastly home-coming. The absence of almost all personal acquaintance with the deceased, and of anything like grief for his loss, together with what had been the inevitable reckoning on his death beforehand, lent a peculiar character to the situation, in which, when the conditions had to do with any

feminine nature less unconquerable than
Miss Janet's, intolerable restlessness and
nameless terror were apt to usurp the fore-
ground. Miss Bethia, even Miss Mackinnon, though her feelings were more shut up
within herself, might well have been forgiven for starting nervously every time the
door opened. In truth, Miss Bethia woke
up half a dozen times during the night, in
spite of the negus which Mr. Mair had con-
siderately brewed and sent up for the ladies,
her hair standing on end, in a bath of per-
spiration, fighting with a nightmare, that
Fenton of Strathdivie had come out of his
coffin in the chamber below, mounted the
stairs and entered her room to ask, as his
servant had done for him, but with an awful
face and gesture, what the Miss Mackinnons
were seeking there.

To the relief of Miss Bethia, if not of
Miss Janet and Miss Mackinnon, who saw
no occasion for the appearance of rival
claimants on the scene, a few gentlemen,

distant relations of the Fentons of Strathdivie, straggled in to occupy the vacant bed-
rooms and represent various branches of the
family at the funeral and the reading of the
will. But the nearest of kin and in affection, as had always been understood, were
unavoidably absent. These were first
cousins on the mother's side, who had been
brought up with the late laird, and had
been his intimate associates all his life, till
they had emigrated to New Zealand several
years back. Thus, the persons who had
most reason to mourn the last of this line
of Fentons would not so much as hear of
his death for many a week, far less have it
in their power to attend his funeral. It was
a still greater comfort to Miss Bethia, and
she believed in her heart to her sisters,
though she did not dare to express her conviction, to wear their long-prepared mourn-
ing, and peep behind the closed window-
blinds at the solemn procession which con-
ducted Fenton of Strathdivie by a bleak

moorland road to his long home. But the
poor woman could hardly appreciate the
advantage of having one burden lifted from
her mind, because of the fever of expectation into which she and the remaining Miss
Mackinnons were thrown with regard to
the removal of another and a lifelong
weight by the reading of the will, which was
to take place on the return of the so-called
mourners.

There was no question of what Jean Mackinnon's marriage settlement had ordained,
but some uncomprehended, undefined power
was supposed to remain in the hands of the
Fenton who was to return the loan which
his house had enjoyed for generations. Besides, the law had many a quirk and quibble,
and was proverbially unchancy. Though
Miss Janet would not allow it to be breathed
for an instant, Miss Bethia had a quaking
fear in her sinking heart that there was still
the risk of a miserable slip between the cup
and the lip, and that she and her sisters

might not only have made fools of themselves, they might be irretrievably ruined—
it was so easy to ruin the last of the Virginian Mackinnons—in the little hold they
had recovered of the world by favour of
Tam Drysdale and Dr. Peter Murray. The
sisters might be rouped out of house and
hold, and the family mansion in St. Mungo's
Square lost to Eneas through the fruitless
journey to Strathdivie, because Miss Janet
had been so strong-willed and high-handed.

In spite of not admitting a doubt of the
result, Miss Janet's sense of honour could
hardly restrain her, in the dreary, torturing
interval of waiting, from taking the law into
her own hands, setting about an instant
search for the will and mastering its contents,
without the help of Mr. Mair or any other
official. Why not, when that clause in Jean
Mackinnon's marriage contract had still to
be fulfilled? But, even if the temptation
had proved too strong to be resisted, in the
absence of all the other connections of the

family, who, being men, had gone in the
van of the friends and neighbours to the
churchyard, the depredation would have been
circumvented by Mrs. Todd, who kept a
vigilant watch over the browbeating, inter-
fering 'auld maid,' dogging her footsteps,
and never losing sight of her. The former
custodian of Strathdivie intercepted and
baffled poor Miss Janet at every point, when
she sought to indemnify herself for the
horrible delay by roaming through the
house and making a mental inventory of all
it contained, including audacious, not surreptitious, efforts to open closed cupboards and
locked drawers.

'That muckle, loud-tongued woman—I
hate the very sicht of her, and I ken the
puir maister would have hated it too—is no
honest.' Mrs. Todd was guilty of a gross
libel on the lady to one of the undertaker's
men engaged to wait at the dinner which
was to follow the funeral.

Miss Janet was perfectly honest, but it

would have been difficult to say to what
Jean Mackinnon's marriage settlement did
not extend in the eyes of her descendants,
unless it were the servants' trunks in their
room, or the strangers' wraps on the hall-
table.

CHAPTER XXVI.

AT last the black-coated company came
back from their melancholy errand, like
soldiers, who on similar occasions exchange
the 'Dead March in Saul' for 'The Roast
Beef of Old England,' interchanging ordinary
talk and gossip all the more briskly for its
temporary suspension, even laughing a little
at passing jests, in undertones. The party
filed into the study—by courtesy—where
they found the three big-boned, hoary-headed
Miss Mackinnons in their places before the
others, seated in three chairs ranged in a
row, as on the sack in the cart which had
brought the sisters to the fateful door of

Strathdivie. But they were not the only women present — considerably to Miss Janet's disgust, Mrs. Todd came in with her husband, and seated herself near the door unforbidden by the lawyer, who was the master of the ceremonies, as he took the chair at the head of the table and produced from the desk at his elbow a paper with black seals, proceeding to read the document with due gravity and emphasis.

The will took most of the people there by surprise—not because it showed Archie Fenton to have been growing more and more an impoverished man. All present, with the exception of the Miss Mackinnons, had used their faculties of observation and become acquainted with that fact. The astonishment was roused by the information that he had not clutched what remained to him of this world's goods to his last moment ; on the contrary, he had used such power as the law gave him to strip himself beforehand of the bulk of his property by

executing a deed of gift in favour of his
cousins in New Zealand—thus putting them
at once in possession of what he had
destined for them, and saving them the payment of legacy-duty. When Archie Fenton
had set his house in order betimes, relieving
a sensitive, nervous mind, and doing his
best to make a dying bed easier, he had
also bought an annuity which provided for
his remaining wants, and spared him the
trouble of disposing of the capital laid
down in the purchase. There were only
two reservations to the course, which had,
perhaps, as much selfishness as justice or
generosity in it. The first had to do with
a moderate bequest to his servants. The
second referred to the claim which the descendants of the Virginian Mackinnons had
on a portion of his estate.

With some elaboration, the late Fenton
of Strathdivie detailed by the lips of the
lawyer the amount of the claim, the manner
in which the money had been originally

laid out, the casualties which had befallen it from time to time, the legal opinion which he had troubled himself to get to certify his exemption from the necessity of refunding these losses—the most of them occurring before his day—the whole suggesting forcibly the tyrannical and vexatious character which the provision for the Mackinnons had ultimately assumed. In the end Fenton, with a vindictive length of memory which the nearness of death had not cut short, imdemnified himself as far as possible for the annoyance he had suffered, by exercising the right of choice which had been left to him, in apportioning, as he saw fit, the two hundred and seventy pounds to which Jean Mackinnon's tocher had dwindled away. To May and Janet Mackinnon, the elder daughters of the late Gavin Mackinnon, of St. Mungo's Square, Glasgow, who, on account of their years, were not likely to derive much benefit from the legacy—a clause framed to deal a double blow to the unfortunate legatees—twenty pounds each. To Elizabeth or Bethia Mackinnon, third daughter of the said Gavin Mackinnon, whom the testator had never seen, whose forward greed had not therefore offended him, whom he judged of an age better suited to profit by any reversion of property —two hundred and thirty pounds.

Miss Janet listened with eyes that glittered like Miss Mackinnon's. Miss Bethia's mouth gaped helplessly.

The next thing which happened was that, without a moment's hesitation, Miss Janet stated plainly to the assembled company :

' It's a shamefu' cheat. Jean Mackinnon's marriage portion maun have been liker ten than twa thousand, let alane hunders ; somebody is answerable for the defalcation.'

' Mem, compose yourself, I beg,' said the lawyer, at whom she glared, speaking with the maddening coolness and politeness of a practised hand in such circumstances.

The audience, which had gathered there without much hope of pecuniary gain, and on that very account found themselves in an easy, disengaged frame of mind, were ready, in the absence of any other source of excitement, to welcome the diversion of listening to an angry woman mulcted of what she believed her due, and, according to a woman's notions, insulted to boot. And not many insulted and aggrieved expectants, even of the female sex, spoke their minds with the refreshing plainness which Miss Janet Mackinnon had already displayed.

'We are willing to make allowance for ruffled feelings'—Mr. Mair again attempted to throw oil on the troubled waters in the storm which had arisen—' but I would warn you, mem, against making vague accusations. It is hard to say to whom your words refer. If it is to the late Mr. Fenton—who has vouchsafed a candid explanation of misadventures over which he had no control, and who, as you have heard, took counsel more than once to satisfy himself that he could not be held responsible for them—although there is a good rule " *de mortuis nil nisi bonum*," I do not pretend that your speech is actionable. But if you have any other person in your mind, I can only repeat to you my advice to be more careful of what you say.'

' What do I care for your advice ony mair than for your writer's Latin ?' cried Miss Janet defiantly. ' You insult the memory of auld Eneas Mackinnon, who, when he was in the body, would have garred [made] every notary-public among you stand about, by lettin' it be said for an instant that his dochter's tocher was a paltry twa or three hunder !'

' Mem, it was two thousand in the beginning—nobody disputes it. But it was badly invested in the sourest land in all the three Wards ; the more's the pity for your sake.'

'Wha are you peetyin' ? Leddies who

are Mackinnons dinna crave pity from men
of business. Keep yours till it is asked for.
What I insist on is that Jean Mackinnon's
tocher had mair chance of being ten than
twa thousand.'

'And what I say, mem, is that the law
takes no account of chances, hardly of probabilities. Can you produce documents to
substantiate your statement?' demanded
Mr. Mair with inflexible gravity, intended
to rebuke the twinkling eyes around
him.

'I daur say no!' said Miss Janet, un-
abashed. 'The Bible says riches have
wings and tak' to flicht, but I think lawyers'
papers maun have as long legs as cowardly
loons of sodgers in a retreat. What is the
use of wulls and contracts, such as my late
nephew Gauvin's marriage contract, when
they vanish like smoke the moment they
are wanted?'

'I have not heard of the casualty,' said
Mr. Mair drily; 'but I thought the office

in Edinburgh was a provision against such
accidents.'

'The Coort of Session!' exclaimed Miss
Janet disdainfully, misunderstanding his
meaning. ' He or she maun be daft, indeed,
wha has recoorse to that refuge. I've
had enough to encounter in my day from
lawyers' gab, but a coortfu' o' them——'

' I'm not sure that one woman would not
be a match for them all,' muttered Mr.
Mair. Then he said in a louder key : ' I
regret, mem, that you have been misin-
formed—I must say it, with regard to your
legacy from Strathdivie, but, at least, it
has not failed your family altogether. Suffer
me to tell you I am not sure that my
friend, the late Mr. Fenton, might not have
successfully contested your claim, and refused to acknowledge it in his will.'

' Oh, Janet,' broke in Miss Bethia, in
desperation, ' say nae mair, lest we lose
what we've got. A bird in the hand, ye
ken, is worth twa in the buss. Twa hunder

and seventy pounds is a gude lump of money, and you are sensible that the only tidin's we could ever pick up about Jean Mackinnon's gear, was that it had maist melted awa', though you would not hear a word to that effect.'

'Haud your tongue, Betheye!' said Miss Janet angrily. 'And what did the man mean by treatin' Meye and me as gin we were superannuate? She's glowerin' at me for word, but somebody else maun write it down for her to read—I have not the heart. Archie Fenton maun hae been daft and no fit to mak' a wull. Even if we had been as auld as the hills, could he not trust us to hand over our shares, when we were done wi' them, to Betheye—our ain sister?'

'There is something to be said there,' admitted Mr. Mair. 'You have ground for complaint on that score. But a lawyer can only act on his instructions, and I must bear witness that Mr. Fenton was in his sound mind when he caused that deed to be drawn up, and when he signed it. Why, it was two years ago, when he was in little worse health than was customary with him.'

'The wull is a whole hatterell [collection] of mistakes,' said Miss Janet doggedly. 'He maun have confused our names, and our standin' in the family.'

' By no means, mem ; you forget that he gives both correctly, and that he mentions Miss Bethia as the third daughter.'

' I wudna believe it, though you were to preach it doon my throat,' maintained Miss Janet.

In such a case there was no more to be said ; but the announcement that dinner was on the table was welcome as putting an end to the discussion.

Then Miss Janet gave way by a hair's-breadth. In place of taking possession of what she wanted as her simple right, she asked Mr. Mair if he had any objection to leave the will, to be looked over by the sisters, and read by Miss Mackinnon.

'No objection in the world,' said the lawyer, courteous by nature, and really willing, as he had been during the whole affair, to do the poor old ladies any service in his power. But it was not business-like for such papers to lie about, so he entrusted Miss Janet with the key of the desk, which contained nothing else of any consequence.

According to old usage in Scotland, the women of the family were not present at the dinner after the funeral—a withdrawal on their part doubtless due in the past to the wild orgies which, like Irish wakes, were wont to establish the respectable standing as well as the hospitable practice of the house, and at once to commemorate the worth of the dead and solace the grief of the male relatives among the living. Such ghastly orgies had long since passed away, but the peculiar reserve which forbade the attendance of women at funerals still made ladies, as a rule, keep their rooms in what was supposed to be the depth of their sorrow. Maiden ladies like the Miss Mackinnons were the last to change old customs.

The three sisters sat still in the room where the will had been read, and after the last man had shut the door behind him, looked in each other's faces. That is, Miss Mackinnon and Miss Janet looked, for poor Miss Bethia, in her innocence, was unable to meet the eyes of the others. She turned away, while Miss Janet did not wait to take possession of the will, but wrote its purport on the slate which had been provided for the enlightenment of Miss Mackinnon. She expressed herself in a feeble version of Miss Janet's passion that it was a cheat and 'havers.'

During the explanation Mrs. Todd came into the room, with a tray for the ladies, and cast a lynx-eye on the desk with the key in it.

The injured women ate and drank— where would have been the gain in letting good food be lost ? Miss Bethia had felt as if every morsel she ate must choke her. But the hotch-potch, roast fowl, and pancakes, which did credit to Mrs. Todd's plain but efficient cookery, were not without a solacing influence, neither were the glasses of Madeira which Mr. Mair had taken care should be added to the meal. What the ladies would have called the generous fare restored some strength to their shaken frames, and with strength came a little reasonableness.

Two hundred and seventy pounds *was* a lump of money. In spite of what might have seemed grasping and avaricious in their natures, the Miss Mackinnons had no right sense of the value of money, any more than if they had been children. The ladies had been poor and growing poorer all their lives. They had even known abject poverty. It was not wonderful that they felt inclined to exaggerate the amount of shillings and pence in two hundred and seventy pounds, and to think they would never come to an

end. The sisters had been startled and deeply
mortified, in the middle of their extravagant
fancies, by the first sound of what the
legacy had dwindled to. After they had
got accustomed to the truth, and had begun
to realize that it was inevitable; after they
had found time to recall what Miss Bethia
had already remembered, of whispers of the
diminution of the property—not listened to
when breathed long before in the Miss Mackinnons' hearing—a change came over the
spirit of their dreams. They commenced
to say to themselves that a little thing was
better than nothing—a great deal better—
that it was not little after all. For two
hundred and seventy pounds was a lump of
money; enough, with what the sisters had
enjoyed lately, to secure them from want
all the days of their lives; nay, even to
enable them to make a 'hochie' (hidden
treasure) for the Lieutenant. With the
wonderful adaptability of human nature—
above all, of woman's nature—the Miss

Mackinnons, including Miss Janet, were remoulding their plans, and reconciling themselves to hundreds instead of thousands, and twos instead of tens. It was no longer the sum itself, it was the heinous injustice and inequality of the division of it, which continued to trouble the ladies. Yet 'it was not lost that a friend got,' and, in their honest family affection, it was possible they would end by not only facing the fact, but by accepting it without a grudge against the favoured individual.

END OF VOL. II.

BILLING AND SONS, PRINTERS, GUILDFORD.

C

www.ingramcontent.com/pod-product-compliance
Lightning Source LLC
Chambersburg PA
CBHW060532030726
47498CB00004B/1166